GW00400233

BE MY TEACHER

EMILY HAYES

1

Rosa Martinez's heart pranced as she stepped through the double-leaf swing door, separating the kitchen from the dining area. Chilly air fleeced across her skin and she exhaled, relieved to be away from the kitchen's heat yet dreading who awaited her.

With hands full of the platter carrying soup bowls, she dutifully swayed her way towards Tomlin's table, careful to avoid bumping into her colleagues, who were equally busy on their feet. Her black apron, gracefully secured around her slender waist, swished with every step she took. She wished he would just leave her alone.

She could feel the sweat from the kitchen still clinging to her forehead, and she moved quicker, eager to have her hands free so that she could wipe the back of her hand across her moist forehead.

"Thank you, Rosa," grinned Tomlin, sitting alone at the two-seater table, "That was pretty fast."

Rosa smiled politely and set down the soup on the placemat before him.

She could feel his deep blue eyes keenly watching her, and she could not help the levels of irritation that spiked through her.

When she straightened up, she maintained her smile like she was trained to do at all times, "Would that be all, sir?"

"Yeah," Tomlin nodded, briefly glancing down at his meal before lifting his gaze back to stare at Rosa's face.

Rosa acknowledged his satisfaction with a nod and turned to leave.

"R-rosa!" Tomlin's stammering voice stopped her in her tracks. She paused, before turning back around to regard his oval face and rounded jaw; many women would consider Tomlin a handsome man, and he was, in all fairness, but she was tired of having him pretentiously come into the restaurant. It wasn't really for the food, she knew, but she didn't know how to make him stop.

"What time are you off today?"

"Same time," she responded, then added, "10:30 pm," as an afterthought. A strand of dark hair escaped from her neatly packed bun and she tucked it behind her ear and shifted her eyes awkwardly to the floor.

"I'll be seated at the bar after dinner," Tomlin cocked his head towards the bar in a short distance. "Please, let me buy you a drink."

"Thank you, but I can't."

He leaned forward on the wood table, adorned with perfectly white tablecloths. "I'm really just trying to get to know you, Rosa," he pleaded, "I-I just want a chance to talk to you."

Tomlin Westbrook was well known around San Francisco; a real estate mogul with hundreds of both commercial and residential properties, with dashing looks that accompanied his success. Many women would kill to be standing in her shoes right now, but Rosa was not impressed by his famous reputation, she had had a busy night and she just wanted to go home to Bailey, and her drafts.

Tomlin was staring at her, imploringly, as if waiting for her to change her mind. She blinked her eyes up to the clock on the wall, *9:50 pm.* "Enjoy your meal, sir." She bowed slightly and hurried away from his presence.

Rosa walked around to the other side of the restaurant where Erin was seated at a corner, cleaning the menus. The restaurant was almost empty now with only Tomlin and two other customers eating. She and Erin would lock up once the customers were finished and paid their checks.

"You really should give him a chance, you know," Erin commented as Rosa took the empty seat opposite hers. "He really likes you. I mean, he's a big deal, Rosa!" she emphasized, widening her eyes and bobbing her head.

Rosa smirked briefly with her eyes dropped. Wordlessly, she reached for the sanitizer, a towel, and an unclean menu book and began to wipe.

Erin rolled her eyes, and shook her head, she could never figure Rosa out. "You're so weird!" she muttered and resumed her cleaning.

AT EXACTLY 11:03PM, Rosa's Toyota drove into her driveway on Balmy Street. One table holding a couple had carried on with hearty conversation while eating extremely slowly and that held her back for longer than usual.

Finally home, she brought the car to a halt and undid her bun, and her thick, wavy, dark hair danced down to the sides of her neck and settled over her shoulders. She reached to the backseat for her sweater; it was January—the coldest month of the year in San Francisco and currently 50 degrees outside. She threw her sweater on over her black company tee-shirt, zipping it up to her neck. Then, she grabbed her sling purse, slipped it over her shoulders, and proceeded to climb out of the car.

She walked briskly towards her studio apartment. As soon as she stepped onto the porch, she could hear Bailey whimpering on the other side of the door. Rosa smiled instinctively—she knew that familiar whimper of joy all too well, and it was a sound she always looked forward to coming home to.

She turned the key in the lock, and when she pushed the door open, Bailey jumped on her. Rosa dropped to her knees chuckling, and the little Portuguese Podengo wagged his brown tail ferociously. Rosa dropped on her back and Bailey climbed on her body as was her custom and began to lick Rosa's face. Rosa laughed heartily, shutting her eyes and tossing her head from side to side, overwhelmed by Bailey's slurpy kisses.

When she finally rose to her feet, she shut the door to her apartment, securing it with the lock. Rosa moved to her kitchen area with Bailey running excitedly after her, with her floppy ears bouncing on the sides of her head.

She reached to her top cabinet and pulled out a pack of Bailey's favorite snacks.

Bailey jumped in circles, already aware of the delicious content that laid within. Rosa sat down on the floor and crossed her legs. One by one, she fed Bailey the Tasty Minis, and she laughed at his antics.

"Okay," Rosa said after several minutes, "That's enough, Bailey."

She put what was left of the treats into the bag and rose to her feet. She replaced them on the cabinet and proceeded to her miniature bedroom.

Rosa felt very proud of her space; the last owner had moved into a bigger house with her fiancée to start a family, and the small apartment became home to her and Bailey.

She avoided clogging the already-small space with too many pieces of furniture, so she kept her decoration as minimalistic as possible. The less items she had in the apartment, the more space she had to move around; not that she needed much of it anyway.

She peeled her purse off her body and flung it to the yellow sofa in the corner. Her bedroom contained that sofa, a queen-sized bed, a desk, and a matching wheeled chair where she sat to do her writing. The desk was small and brown, with an extra shelf at the top where she kept her organizational caddy and a file holder.

The file holder housed her important papers and documents while her pens, and pencils were stashed in the caddy, along with her stationary and all other office supplies.

She had small photographs of the most important people in her life pinned to the rectangular caddy. There was a photograph of her and Bailey taken on one of their numerous walks in the park, then there was one taken at a Thanksgiving dinner with her sister and their mother, who now lived in Seattle with her new husband. The third was a photograph of Max Moore, a successful lesbian author whose work Rosa was nearly obsessed with.

She had printed Max's photograph off the internet and placed it on the upper layer of her desk to serve as an inspiration and a reminder of where she wanted to be in the next few years of her career.

Bailey hopped onto the bed as Rosa changed into her pink and black pajamas.

She gathered the day's clothes in her arms and strolled into the kitchen where she dropped them in the washer to wash overnight.

Then, she collected a glass from the wine glass holder and grabbed a bottle of New Age Red, she poured herself a glass and walked back into her bedroom, which also served as an office. She sat down at her desk and flipped open her MacBook.

While she waited for the system to boot, she drank from her glass in small sips.

Bailey jumped on her lap and she scratched his neck playfully. "Mama's gotta write, Bailey," she informed the unconcerned dog, who had missed her too much to care.

2

Max Moore languidly held a sleeping Emma under her black silk sheets. She didn't usually do this, cuddling was not her thing, yet Emma's pretty face was resting on Max's small firm breasts and her long golden hair spread over Max's arm. Max didn't have so much choice in it.

It was six in the morning and the sun had risen outside her Victorian home, with the morning rays illuminating her large bedroom, but Emma was still in her bed. This was never the idea, she was not supposed to spend the night, and as much as Max didn't appreciate having her sleep over

—worse, in her arms—she could not bring herself to kick her out into the cold last night, especially not after the bottle of wine they had consumed and the intense fucking that took place afterward by her fireplace.

Emma is only 23! Max mentally shook her head at herself for this one. She was drawn to the younger women, but this was pushing it—even by her own standards. She needed to choose more carefully in future.

Max stretched her free hand sideways and felt the white and gold nightstand for her glasses. When she finally touched them, she picked them up and brought them to her eyes. She gave one last look at Emma before carefully pulling free from underneath her. Emma cooed in her sleep and shifted in the bed, undisturbed.

Max mumbled something under her breath.

She planted her strong legs to the tiled floor and stretched her hands over her head until she could hear the bones crack in her back. Then, she cracked her neck and matched into her luxurious bathroom.

Max looked at her naked body in the mirror. She felt every year of her forty five years but she enjoyed that it still didn't tell in her body. She trained every day in the gym to keep her strong physique.

Max cleaned her teeth then turned the faucet off and reached for a towel.

"Hey..." Emma, said, coming up behind her, naked. She wrapped her tiny arms around Max's waist and pressed the side of her head to her back. "Good morning." Her voice was warm and sensual.

When Max saw that the girl was not going to unclasp her hands from around her waist, she dropped her hands down to her sides and turned around to face her, relaxing down against the sink.

"Look, Emma, I had a great time last night, it was beautiful, you're beautiful," Max emphasized with an open palm, "help yourself to a shower and I will order you an uber. I need to work."

"What?" Emma's eyes widened. "I thought... I thought this was the beginning of—"

"Nothing. This was not the beginning of anything, I did tell you this before we met and then again last night. No strings. A bit of fun. Nothing serious. You know that, baby." she shook her head matter-of-factly.

Tears welled up in Emma's eyes and Max watched her, unmoved. "I need to work," Max reminded her.

"Fine!" Emma finally found her voice. "You're probably gonna die alone! Don't order me anything, I will sort myself out." With that, she turned around and marched into the bedroom.

She ran down the u-shaped stairs to the fireplace where her jeans and tank top had been yanked to the floor by Max's eager hands last night. Max was still at the sink upstairs, straining her ears to the distant sounds of Emma's movements in the front room downstairs. She imagined her angrily pulling her clothes on and roughly snatching her bag from the hanger by the door.

"Go away!" Emma shouted as Diablo, Max's big black dog, began to bark.

It wasn't long before Max heard a bang of the front door; so loud, it reminded her of the others that had gone before Emma. *They always leave so angrily. Even though I never promise them anything, I am always honest. They always hope for more.*

She headed out of the bathroom to be met by Diablo. She ruffled the hair on his head and smiled at him. "You and me still, boy."

Max walked into her closet and picked a set of black gym clothes from her neatly organized drawer where Magda, the house-keeper, had placed it. *She always does such a good job with organizing my stuff.*

She pulled the clothes onto her firm body, followed by a matching sneaker; she liked to wear black. A lot of her wardrobe was plain in denim or black.

She grabbed a face towel and followed the wood-railing staircase down into the basement that served as her gym. It was her sanctuary and she had had it beautifully done out with full sets of weights, a bench, a pull up rig and squat rack and a bike and treadmill.

Max climbed the treadmill, turned on the Bluetooth on her phone, and waited for it to connect to the speakers inside her gym.

Instead of music, she played a story submitted by one of the numerous writers who usually sent in works to the office. Max Moore, aside from being a renowned and award winning author, had set up her own publishing business which had been hugely successful. She put many hours into discovering new talent and getting them ready to publish. Using a text-to-speech application on her phone, she pressed start before placing her phone down.

She began a warm up jog, whilst listening to the misplaced words and terrible grammar of whoever wrote that latest piece of shit.

osa jumped up, startled.

She scrambled for her phone, shakily swiped at the green button, and slapped the device to her ear. "He-hello?" her voice was grumpy and inaudible.

"Were you still sleeping?"

Rosa scratched at her eyes. "Hi, Mom."

"Did you fall asleep on your computer again?"

Bailey barked at Rosa's feet and Rosa leaned forward to scratch the dog's head. "I was working on my book," she explained tiredly.

"My poor baby. Well, don't you worry,

okay? I'm sure they'll simply love your work—"

"Mom, WordFlux rejected my manuscript before." She ran a tired hand through her messy dark hair.

"Well, that was a first effort," insisted the optimistic mother. "I'm sure it will be different this time around."

"I just really want to be given a chance, you know?" She had walked into WordFlux that day, nervously excited, with her tan fingers hanging on to her green turquoise backpack that had her manuscript tucked inside. The secretary had collected the manuscript, promising to deliver it to the publisher. Five months later, she got an email telling her to try again another time. Rosa heaved heavily at the memory...

"I know," her mother was saying at the other end of the phone, "And you will. Just, try not to fall asleep on your desk anymore, your neck could cramp, Rosa."

"I know, Mama" she instinctively raised her right hand to rub the side of her neck. "How's Thomas?" she asked of her stepfather. Rosa had not spent much time around him, but from her infrequent visits to their suburban home, she could tell that he made her mama happy and that was enough for her.

"He's great!" her mother cooed, and she could imagine her smiling at the other end of the phone. "He's taking me to Hawk Hill this weekend! "

"Good for you, Mama."

"You know," her mother's voice went low, and Rosa knew exactly what she would say next.

"Mom," she stopped her before she could begin with her usual sermon, "I'm busy with work."

"Which is why you should take a break to go on dates!" Her voice was insistent. "I'm sure there are great young Spanish men in San Francisco. Put yourself out there, honey, your life cannot continue to revolve around your dog and that author you keep breaking your neck to please—"

"Max Moore, Ma, her name is Max Moore."

"Yeah, well, put yourself out there! Do something else, you're twenty-eight now, allow your heart to find love, baby, and who knows, I might just see grandkids in my lifetime."

"Thanks, Mom."

"Think about it, Rosa,"

"I love you, Mom,"

"And call your sister!"

"Bye, Mom." Rosa ended the call.

Lola, Rosa's older sister, was an extrovert; loud and outgoing, she lived in Miami where she had a thriving career as a news anchor and spent whatever free time she had discreetly frolicking under the sheets with younger men.

On her own, Rosa called her sister twice a week except for when Lola decided to bombard her with calls, of which she didn't always pick up.

She was not the best conversationalist anyway, never had been, and she expected her family more than anyone else to be fine with that by now. She always felt closer to dogs than people.

"Come on, Bailey!" she called to the waiting dog as she stood up. Let's get you some breakfast and get out for a walk."

Bailey jumped excitedly, recognising

her favorite words. Rosa smiled at her little best friend and got ready to head out.

ROSA'S HEART WAS DETERMINED, she was going to rewrite her book so well, Max Moore would have no choice but to get her published. This was what she lived for, it's all she'd dreamt about in the past few years of her life.

She had first come across Max's most successful novel, Amanda's Summer on the shelves of her local bookstore. It had a strong lesbian main character and the storyline was definitely a lesbian romance with more depth and layers than Rosa had ever read before. Max's book was so good it had won mainstream awards which was so unusual for a lesbian story.

Rosa had not been able to stop reading. The book was long and had kept her up all night.

Mesmerized by the author who had created this masterpiece, Rosa became keen to know more about her, and like all books, a sketchy biography of Max was printed inside the back page of the novel.

Max Moore had swept her off her feet; her entrapping play on words and the unique storyline was unlike anything she had ever read before. She was a fan—had become an instant fan—and like all fans, she would haunt her idol and immerse herself into anything and everything Max Moore.

Thanks to the internet, with just a few clicks Rosa was faced with plenty of information on Max Moore. The Google page told her who Max Moore was, what city she lived in, her successful publishing business, WordFlux, more photographs of her, video interviews, and mentioned her ex-wife, Caroline.

Rosa watched Max in the videos, her strong shoulders, short hair, the set of her jaw and her bold features. Rosa mostly watched those deep dark brown eyes that were almost black and sparkled with an intensity that blew Rosa away.

Wikipedia went further to mention all her published books and Rosa made sure to order them all off Amazon. And she read them, not one was left unfinished. As an aspiring writer herself, she felt connected to Max's style of writing, and while Max rarely published lesbian romance, *Amanda's Summer* remained Rosa's favorite of all her works; the book was a first love affair for Rosa.

Thoughts of the draft back on her desk and what she needed to do to get approval from Max Moore raced across Rosa's mind, as she went for a jog with Bailey. A man working on the corner of the park whistled as she ran past, and she wished momentarily she hadn't worn the short shorts. She still had a good number of hours before it was time to start her shift at the restaurant and she was going to utilize that precious time to get home and get some work done on her novel.

Tired, she screeched to a halt and dropped her hands forward on her knees, breathless. Rosa wasn't much of an athlete, she didn't run for miles, but she loved to go out for twenty minutes most days. Running helped her collect her thoughts and get her pumped for the day. Plus, Bailey loved it.

She looked sideways at Bailey who had

taken advantage of her stop to wander off, sniffing into the ground. "Come on! Bailey!" she called to the dog who abandoned her quest and scampered after her owner.

"Hi, Mr. Rodriguez!" Rosa waved at her neighbor as she ran up to her front door. Mr. Rodriguez was dutifully pushing the electric mower over his lawn with large headphones over his ears. Rosa flashed him a smile like she always did, and the older man acknowledged her greeting with an equally warm smile, waving back at her.

She disappeared into her apartment and walked straight to her bathroom. She stepped out of her running clothes and tossed them into the laundry basket, then stepped into the shower and turned the faucet on. She stood naked under the warm water, enjoying the feeling of it running over her body.

Her nipples grew hard from the water's caress. She covered her sponge in shower gel and began to wash herself, she loved being alone in the hot shower. Might even more fun being with someone in the hot shower.

She shut her eyes and put her head

under the water thinking again of Max Moore. She wished the woman would just dedicate her precious time to reading her work, even if it were just a part of it.

But she still had a chapter to go, and an epilogue to follow up with.

Would it be a better idea to approach Max directly outside of the publishing house rather than going through official channels?

She pondered whether that would give her a greater chance.

4

"Now, you listen to me, Ava!" Max Moore yelled angrily into her phone as she sat relaxed in her office chair. "When I make a decision on a draft, it is final. I do not have the time to go through the same script over and over again, do you understand me?!"

Max worked from her home office often. She loved her beautiful home and she spent as much time as possible in it.

"Yes, ma'am," the secretary spoke from the other end of the phone.

"Whatever manuscript had been rejected the first time should not be accepted by you or anyone at the office. Do I make myself clear?"

"Yes, ma'am."

"If they couldn't get it right the first time, they won't get it right the second time." Her voice trailed off as she muttered the last sentence, more to herself than to Ava. She punched her screen hard and dropped the phone on her desk.

She was stressed.

Every waking day, she had to read manuscripts from wannabe writers, and some of them were garbage, the garbage that gave her a bad headache, now someone was trying to submit a rejected script for a second time, and there was no way she was going to condone that! It didn't matter that the rejection email always asked them to check back at another time—that was a mere pleasantry.

By *check back* she meant, write another story, a fucking better one this time, goddammit!

She lifted her palm to her forehead and scowled. Her head hurt, plus, she was irritated by the young writers she had seen lately.

Just a whole bunch of lazy sloths! She swore under her breath then rose heavily from the chair and made her way to the mini-fridge in the corner. She grabbed a bottle of vodka and poured a big shot into a glass. She added a small amount of Coca Cola. It burned her throat as she swallowed it, and she exhaled audibly, shaking her head to clear away the infuriating thoughts of the activities going on at WordFlux.

One final gulp and she replaced the bottles back in the fridge, turned around and headed back to her large mahogany desk.

She sat down and the silence hit her. She had such a big beautiful house and the only voices ever present were hers and Diablo's. She always claimed that she loved the quietness—and she did; just, sometimes, it was a bit too quiet... and lonely.

If only Caroline...

She shook her head to shake away the thoughts then sighed deeply and redirected her attention to the open Word document in front of her.

"**G**uess what!" Lola screamed excitedly into the phone.

Rosa cringed at the deafening loudness.

She had just typed in the last sentence of her book, saved it on her flash drive, and was flopped back in her chair, exhausted and apprehensive about what to do next. "You'll tell me even if I don't ask," she muttered.

"Max Moore works from home and I found out where she lives!"

Rosa jumped to her feet. Curiosity quickly replacing her exhaustion.

"We had this special guest on the show,

a *very* handsome guy—" Rosa could hear her sister swooning down the phone.

"Get on with it, Lola!"

"Fine!" Lola responded, and Rosa imagined her rolling her eyes but she didn't care.

"Anyway, we got talking and he mentioned that the Max Moore was actually his neighbor before he moved away from Pacific Heights—and I said, the novelist and publisher Max Moore?- and he said, thats the one- and I said, OMG my little sister is OBSESSED with her..."

"Oh my god! Lola! What street, house number?"

"Relax!"

"What's the house number, Lola? C'-mon!" Rosa's feet were pacing the floor, edgily excited.

"117 Beaumont Avenue, but don't tell her where you got it from—"

"I love you so much!" Rosa blurted into the phone and cut the call.

She scribbled the address quickly on the yellow sticky note on her desk, and gathered her laptop into her backpack, along with the notepad and flash drive. Rosa snatched her purse, car keys, and phone, then dashed for the door only to swerve back at Bailey's inquisitive bark. "I'll be right back!" She kissed the dog quickly and made a run for the door.

Once in the car, she typed the address into her Google maps and set the phone on the dashboard phone holder.

Fifteen minutes to her destination, she observed from the phone's screen.

All this while, it had only been 15 minutes to Max Moore's house!

Rosa smiled triumphantly to herself as the car hurtled down the road.

Her palms were sweating with her excitement, and her heart thumped in her chest. This was a little crazy she thought briefly and perhaps a little stalkerish, but nevertheless she needed to do it more than anything else. She needed to meet Max Moore face to face.

Fatigued from reading drafts all morning, Max peeled herself from her desk and languidly strolled out of the office. Diablo was laying by the door in the hallway and Max crouched to the floor and scratched the dog's neck lovingly. Diablo lifted his chin and pushed his face into Max's hand.

"Sometimes I miss her, you know?" she spoke to the dog, "I mean, I know I shouldn't, not after what she did but there are days..." her eyes became fixated on the floor and her words trailed off as memories came rushing back to her. "Some quiet days," she sighed, "that I think about her, and the way she used to be..."

Diablo inched forward and licked her face, shaking her out of her thoughts, and Max smiled and hugged the big dog.

Ding dong! The doorbell sounded, and Diablo jumped up barking.

Ding dong! The bell repeated itself and Max's brows furrowed into a frown.

Who could that be? She wasn't expecting anyone.

Ding dong! It repeated, and she fumed at the frequency of the ring. Diablo continued to bark and the dog hopped after Max as she made her way towards the front door, she was pissed. She hated being disturbed at home.

She pulled the large door open and was faced with a young woman with a cloud of long dark hair and big brown eyes. The woman gasped under her breath, "Max Moore!"

"May I help you!" Max asked, eyeing her up and down. Max couldn't help her eyes trailing over the woman's body. Her breasts weren't huge but they were near enough popping out of her loose fitting yellow summer dress.

She climbed a step further up the porch stairs and extended her right hand to Max. "I'm Rosa Martinez."

However attractive this girl was, Max was still unhappy about the approach to her home. Max spent a lot of time alone and she liked it that way. Rosa retreated one step down, pushing her dark hair behind her ears. Max liked the way it fell messily over her collarbone.

"I don't take visitors to my home without appointment."

Rosa dropped her eyes to the floor and stood still like a lamb taken to the slaughter.

"What do you want? Why are you here?" Max stayed firm.

"I just," Rosa spoke with her head bowed, "I ju-just really wanted to meet you. I...I a-am a huge fan," she shrugged, then suddenly, as if awoken by some force, she sprung her face up and gazed back into Max's eyes. "I think your work is incredible and I know," she paused a hand in the air,

"I know you've heard this a thousand times before but you really, *really* write amazingly."

Max fixed her gaze.

"You had no right to show up like this," Max finally stated, the loathing clear in her voice and posture.

"I know and I'm so—"

"Leave!" And Diablo gnashed his teeth from behind his owner as if to emphasize their unacceptance of Rosa.

Rosa ignored Diablo and stood her ground, determined. Max's brow furrowed in surprise.

"Please," Rosa pleaded, tears gathering up in her eyes, "I've lived for this moment right here and right now. I can't go." She shook her head and a tear escaped onto her cheek. "Please, ma'am, just have a look at my work... I know I am still raw, but I am passionate and dedicated to becoming the best writer I can be. I'll do whatever it takes."

Rosa looked around her searchingly and quickly dipped a hand into her back-pack and pulled out her flash drive.

Holding it forward, she took a step up the stairs, and Diablo growled again at her. Rosa regarded the dog only for a split second before taking a second step that brought her right in front of Max.

Max felt Rosa's delicate feminine presence in front of her. Rosa was shorter than Max by only a couple of inches which was unusual in itself because Max was tall and women were usually a lot shorter than her. However Rosa was all long thin legs and arms like a young foal. Max watched her breasts as they rose and fell. Max could smell her perfume and it smelt sweet and floral. This girl looked like a model. What was she doing asking to have her writing read?

"Please," she pleaded earnestly, "just one page. Please, I'll do anything." Max enjoyed watching this beautiful girl begging. For a second her mind moved to filthy thoughts and she shook her head to shake them away.

"Fine!" Her voice was firm, but that was good enough for Rosa and she smiled gratefully.

As Max reached to take the device from her, their fingers brushed and Rosa's cheeks flushed. She pushed some hair behind her ear and took two steps down the stairs.

"Just one chapter," Max warned her before withdrawing into the building and shutting the door in Rosa's face.

Rosa turned around in slow motion, cupped her hands over her mouth, and screamed inaudibly, bouncing on her feet.

MAX WATCHED Rosa from behind her drapes, the young woman made her way to her car and was standing by her car on the phone smiling. Max observed Rosa attentively, the way her short yellow dress just covered her ass and her hips swayed as she walked. The way her long tan legs looked hellishly sexy and slightly awkward at the same time. How incredibly beautiful she looked when she smiled.

God. Max. Take a cold shower.

She had never felt anything like this before, not even when she first met Caroline at that formal dinner event. Now here she stood, hiding behind her curtain like a little kid to watch the beautiful stranger who showed up minutes ago on her front porch.

She had been blown away when she opened her door and beheld Rosa's face and her body as she stood there on her doorstep in that short dress exposing those smooth tan thighs.

And then her smile that was so lovely, but Max had still found a way to be miserable to her.

How old was she?

This is crazy. It is lust, Max. Pure lust for another pretty young thing. You just liked her because she said she would do anything. Pull yourself together.

The tires of Rosa's car screeched against the road as she suddenly pulled away. Max closed the curtain and moved towards her home office, suddenly feeling a burst of energy.

She sat down at her desk and inserted the flash drive into her system.

A well-margined cover page carrying the title with Rosa's full name, email, and phone number greeted her eyes, and she clicked the arrow button to take her to the first page of the first chapter. She relaxed into her high-back executive chair and in ten minutes, she was scrolling through the 10th page of the book.

7

R osa was still in high school when she sat in the hallway of the ER, waiting and watching as the doctors rushed in and out of the room where her cousin Isabella was laboring in anguish. Rosa thought she would faint for she had never felt that scared in her life before. They were both only sixteen, and Isabella, her fragile cousin and only close friend who could not even withstand the sting of injection was battling to bring a baby into the world. Rosa felt nervous, unable to sit still amongst their family, she paced the floor, cringing and pressing her palms to her ears to shut out the heartbreaking wails of Izzy.

That was what it felt like as Rosa moved around the restaurant that evening, waiting on tables.

Her book was with Max.

Would she read it? If she did read it, when would she read it? And if she did read it at all, would she like it? And if she likes it, would she call her?

Maybe her storyline was silly and unrealistic, maybe her writing came across as flat. Maybe Max wouldn't get beyond the first line...

Her heart worried with questions and her hands trembled with anticipation and when she stood to take a customer's order, the pen slipped from her hand onto the floor and she bumped her forehead hard against the table as she bent over to pick it up. The table moved with the force and Rosa yelped. She never got any less clumsy particularly when distracted.

"Hey, are you okay?" the concerned customer, a man in his late thirties, asked her, rising to his feet.

"I'm fine," she replied, rubbing her forehead.

Her manager, Mr. Pablo, sighted the commotion and walked up to the table. "Is everything okay here?" he asked, darting eyes between Rosa and the customer.

"She bumped her head," the concerned customer explained, still standing on his feet.

"I'm fine," Rosa insisted reaching her fingers up to her forehead and feeling sticky blood.

"You should get an ice pack for that," the customer recommended. "You don't want it swelling into a bump."

"Why don't you take a break, Rosa. Get some ice on that and then go home. You can finish early." the manager suggested, which Rosa knew was actually a direct order. "Erin will take it from here."

"Okay, sir." She turned around and walked away with a palm to her forehead. She overheard Mr. Pablo apologizing to the customer.

~

ROSA OPENED the door to her apartment and was greeted by a jumping Bailey, "Hi,

Bailey!" She stepped into the house and shut the door behind her, holding an ice pack to her forehead.

She had picked it from the fridge at work and had to drop it on the car seat to drive. On arriving home, she picked it up and placed it back to her forehead.

Bailey barked, concerned, and she dropped to her knees to hug the dog. "It's okay, Bailey, it's just a little bump. C'mon!"

They moved into the bathroom area and she looked at herself in the mirror, moving the ice pack away to gently touch the swelling. "Ow!"

It still hurt.

Her phone vibrated and she dropped the ice pack in the sink and reached into the bag still across her shoulders. It was an unknown number. "Hello?"

"I read your work," said the voice at the other end and Rosa immediately recognized the voice.

"Max," she murmured.

"You have some potential, but I'm afraid it's not good enough."

Rosa's body shook. She pushed her

hand down on the sink to keep herself from falling. "I could learn from you," she blurted, determined to maximize the rare opportunity of finally having Max's attention. "I could be your student—"

"I don't take on students."

"An assistant! I could do any work you don't want to do- housework or admin work. I'm a great dog walker. I could work for you for free in exchange for you teaching me." she insisted. "Please give me a chance. I could be better, I will be better if I just stay under your watch, *please*, ma'am."

Max was silent on the other end of the phone, and Rosa shut her eyes and waited. Her lips shook and she mouthed *please, please, please.*

"Fine. I'll find some work for you." Max finally said, and Rosa's eyes popped open, her feet jumped for joy. "My house, 9 am, Monday."

"Thank you, thank you soooo much!" she screamed and the phone line cut.

"Yes! Yes!!" Rosa jumped in the air, suddenly forgetting her swollen forehead and the ice pack melting in the sink. "We made

it, Bailey, we made it. I knew I moved to this
town for an excellent reason!" She dropped
to the floor and Bailey jumped on her body,
and she laughed and tickled the barking
dog.

ROSA LOOKED AT THE TIME. It was 7.30. She
knew she could get to the store before it
closed at 8.

She walked to the store located a few
blocks away from her apartment and slid
into the brightly lit building. There was
music playing in the background and customers trooping in and out of the busy
store, chattering and laughing loudly.

Rosa grabbed a basket by the door and
made a turn into the women's department.
She wanted something to wear for Max.
Something about her was desperate to
make a good impression. She picked up a
couple of her usual style loose fitting short
dresses and some shirts.

"Thank you," she smiled at the lady behind the counter who handed her card
back to her.

"Have a nice day," the lady called after her.

"And you too," replied Rosa.

8

Monday morning, Max woke up a few minutes earlier than she normally did. She felt unusually excited.

Diablo was just by the stairs as she headed down and Max took a moment to rub the big dog. Hopping down the stairs, the dog followed after her and they both walked into her kitchen. She made herself a cup of espresso coffee, kept it on the sink to cool, then made up Diablo's food and let him out into the yard with his breakfast.

As the dog ate, she stood by the sink and drank her coffee in small sips. Her thoughts drifted towards Rosa, the skinny dark-haired Hispanic girl; she hadn't really stopped thinking about her ever since she showed up unannounced on her front porch.

Now she wondered how and why she accepted to have her come into her home so easily, and serve as her assistant.

She hadn't had an assistant in her home office before because she never needed one. The only other person that came around her house so frequently was Magda, her housekeeper, and she came around three times a week to clean and tend to Diablo. But, as far as her official work was concerned, all her employees worked in the head office at WordFlux, every single one of them. They communicated with her from there and she corresponded from her home office, only going to the head office rarely.

So, this was new for her; she felt surprised in herself. Surprised at how Rosa got her to agree to have her under her roof.

She had made a couple of Google searches, but there wasn't much about her out there except for her Facebook and Instagram pages, which didn't show much— weird for a girl like her, Max had thought.

Young women Rosa's age lived on and for social media, but the girl didn't have a presence. Particularly with her face and body, Max was expecting multiple posed selfies. Instead there were a lot of photos of a small dog, a couple of group shots of her with what looked like family and that was about it.

Max sighed out loud. She drank what was left of the coffee in one gulp and set the mug down on the countertop.

She walked out and made a turn into her basement. Inside her basement, she played a script on her Read Aloud software, then moved to her weight bench and started some warm up sets.

In 40 minutes, Rosa would be here...

THE TRAFFIC WAS as light as could be, making way for Rosa's Camry as she drove down the highway. The weather was beautiful and Rosa was as excited as a teenager at a block party.

"Siri, call Isabella," she commanded the

intelligent virtual assistant and waited as the phone rang on the other end.

"Hola!"

"You sound excited," observed Isabella.

"I am," Rosa admitted, "but I'm nervous too."

"Don't be," Isabella said, already aware of Rosa's new job as an assistant. "You're smart, I'm sure Max will warm up to you—"

"She was so cold, Izzy, she's like totally intimidating, I almost peed myself."

Both women laughed.

"But I liked it," Rosa subtly admitted. "She's all big and tough looking and muscular. I kind of liked that mean look of hers."

"Well, see? There's something!"

"I mean, she's Max Moore, what's not to love, right?"

"Exactly! Hey! Step away from the television!"

Rosa laughed, "Is that Antonio?"

"I swear he gets on my nerves sometimes," she said, and Rosa could imagine her rubbing a tired palm across her forehead.

"Well, good thing he has a big brother to look up to, right? Miguel will teach him everything he needs to know, and I'm sure he helps out around the house too."

"When he is not locked up in his room, you mean?"

"He still has those mood swings?"

"I swear, Rosa, I can't keep count any more."

Rosa laughed, "Well, he's becoming a teenager; it's pretty normal for them to act out at this age."

"Yeah," Isabella acknowledged. "He's become fond of this new girl in his class."

"Aww!"

"They're inseparable. I go to all their ball games, they're so cute."

"He is a fine young man. He'll have more of those as he grows, blame it on your good genes, and Mateo's."

Isabella chuckled.

"Okay, I have to go; I'm pulling up at her place now"

"Good luck! Try not to pee yourself!"

"I'll need it. I'll text you later, bye!"

"Bye, mama."

Rosa brought her car to a halt in Max's driveway and the nerves returned.

She exhaled, willing herself to relax.

You can do this. You can do this, Rosa.

She shut her eyes, pinned her fingers together, and took a long breath. She held it in then exhaled loudly, opening her eyes.

Feeling better, she snatched her cross-body bag from her passenger's seat and proceeded to get out of the car.

As her feet touched the ground, she breathed in the morning's gentle breeze, taking a second to let it blow through her hair. She tucked her hair behind her ears and marched to Max's porch. She climbed up the short stairs and rang the doorbell then glanced down at her wristwatch—she was ten minutes early.

MAX COULD SEE her from where she was seated in her office. Her office was downstairs, to the right from the entrance, just after the anteroom. The large office had a clear window that overlooked her lawn, and she could see everything from where she was seated when she had the drapes pulled to the side. And that morning, she had them pulled in one direction, giving her ample space to be able to see Rosa walking up to her lawn.

She wore a floaty short dress again in lavender this time with white sandals. Her skin, as smooth as butter, glowed under the morning sun. Her dress swirled from side to side as she walked, her hair was dark and shiny, falling down over her shoulders and Max could not resist the lump that grew in her throat.

She swallowed hard.

A second ring of the doorbell caused Max to rise to her feet, setting her cup of coffee down on her table.

She could hear the door open and Magda and Rosa's voices were audible as they exchanged pleasantries.

"This way," invited Magda, "She's expecting you."

They would be here in seconds.

Max glanced at her face quickly through her wall mirror, satisfied with the sharpness of her face yet feeling stupid for caring what she looked like so much this morning, and backed away from the mirror and turned around just as a knock came on the door.

"Come in!" she responded.

The two women walked through the door.

"Thank you, Magda, I'll take it from here."

Magda nodded and smiled, retracing her steps out of the room. She shut the door behind her, leaving Rosa and Max standing on the floor of her office.

9

"Wow!" Rosa exclaimed, breaking the silence. Her eyes roamed across the vast room with her hands clasped down in her thighs. "Your office is beautiful," she remarked.

"Yeah, thanks." Max regained herself, her throat suddenly feeling parched.

She took two strides forward and extended a hand to Rosa. Rosa took her hand and goosebumps crept up Max's arms. Rosa's fingers were long and delicate. Her nails were neatly manicured, short and painted in a pale pink. "It's good you like it since you'll be spending so much time here," she said, withdrawing her hand. She moved away to stand by the window.

"Thank you so much, Ms. Moore," Rosa spoke back, "I'm honored to have this opportunity and I promise you will not regret it—"

"It's what you all say."

"This would be different, ma'am, I assure you."

She glanced over her shoulder to regard the young woman staring at her wide-eyed with all the sincerity in the world. "Hmph!"

"I promise, I'll do anything you need me to do. I'm very capable." Rosa insisted as Max moved away from the window.

She went around her large desk and collapsed into the chair with her hands sprawled across the armrests. Changing her position, she sat back up and leaned forward on the desk, holding her hands up to her chin. "We'll see," she said to an obviously nervous Rosa. She enjoyed Rosa's nerves. She enjoyed the flush on Rosa's face and her downcast eyes.

Max shifted her eyes to a corner of the room and tipped her chin in the same direction. "You'll sit over there."

Rosa turned and looked at the desk sitting to her right-hand side.

This L-shaped desk was made of white gloss marble with gold-plated legs and a chair. It sat at the other end of the room, carefully planned so Max could watch her easily but she would have to turn her head to the side to see Max. Ahead of her was a blank wall with her eyes in full view of the front door.

"Thank you," Rosa said.

"Sit, your job starts now."

Rosa smiled and moved obediently towards the desk. As she walked past, Max caught a glimpse of her ass, small and hidden behind her flimsy dress, yet round enough to give Max a silhouette and many ideas.

She blinked her eyes away.

"How old are you, Rosa?"

"Twenty-eight," she responded from her new desk. She was standing over the marble desk, setting the items from her bag down on the top.

Twenty-eight, a bit too young for me... Not that I haven't had younger.

Max rolled her eyes at her own thoughts.

When Rosa finished setting her desk, she walked to Max and stood in front of her. "I'm ready to begin, Ms. Moore. Is there something I can do right now?"

Impressed, yet too guarded to let her know, she said, "So, this is how this is going to work, you'll do some work for me and in return, I'll help you with your writing."

"What sort of work, ma'am?"

"Whatever work I say. You said you could do anything, right?" she stated firmly and enjoyed the nervous flush in Rosa's cheeks. The young woman had been nervous ever since she stepped through her door. Max felt her confidence come right back.

"Okay," agreed Rosa.

"Now, go walk Diablo. Magda will put him on a leash and you can walk him around the neighborhood. Don't wander off too far. He mostly doesn't like people so don't take it personally. He is grumpy but he won't bite or anything. Don't let him off the leash anywhere."

"Yes, ma'am."

"Don't be gone for more than thirty minutes, and when you're back, make me a cup of coffee. Magda would show you the way."

"Yes, ma'am." She pushed her hair behind her ears and walked out of the office.

She met Magda in the kitchen, narrated her task to the housekeeper, and watched as the elderly woman put a black harness around Diablo. When the harness was properly secured, she attached a leash to the two rings located right above the buckle.

The dog was grumpy like her owner, but this was a comfortable area for Rosa, she had been around dogs long enough to understand their body language.

"He only looks intimidating," Magda assured her, "He's a sweet boy!"

Patiently harnessing the skills she had learned from dealing with dogs over the years, Rosa crouched to the floor and kept her hands to her sides. Diablo moved forward to sniff her and Rosa remained still on the ground as the dog sniffed around her in circles.

"See? He's warming up to you already," smiled Magda.

Rosa smiled sweetly at the woman, then she reached out her hand to gently pat the dog.

~

"WHAT'S UP, ROSA?" Lola's voice rang as loudly as a bird in its usual manner. "How's it going over there?"

"Fine," Rosa spoke into the phone. "I'm walking Diablo—"

"Diablo, is that a dog?"

"Yeah," Rosa smiled, eyeing the dog who was walking in front of her, grateful that the dog was not pulling on his leash.

"She sent you to walk her dog!"

"It's fine, he's really adorable. At first, he wouldn't stop gnashing at me, but Magda stepped in to—"

"Who's Magda?"

"Max's housekeeper?"

"Oh!"

"Yeah. So anyway, Diablo is warming up to me now."

"She better get your manuscript pub-lished after all this."

"It's a process, Lola."

"Well, you're good at what you do! She better not turn you to a maid, Rosa. Has she got you making her coffee as well?"

"I did that yesterday on my first day."

"Oh, lord!"

"And I'll do that again right after I get Diablo home."

"Girl!"

"I'm not complaining."

"Fine, well," she paused before continu-ing, "I love you"

"I love you too, bye." The call ended. "C'mon, Diablo, that's enough for today."

Rosa walked Diablo back into Max's house. She led the dog to the kitchen and gave him some of his dry biscuits.

While the dog ate, Rosa boiled Max's coffee.

How little people know of each other, she thought as her mind wandered.

At first, she had admired Max Moore from a distance—worshipped her actu-ally! And she still did in some way; the woman was brilliant, she was Max Moore, for God's sake! But these two days with her had been nothing like Rosa had hoped they would be. Max was grumpy and even harsh; it was almost as if Rosa's very presence irritated her. It made Rosa wonder, what was she doing wrong? She refused to believe that anyone would be born that bitter. There was something, and that something was obviously eating at Max...

She shook her head to shake away the thoughts.

I better mind my own business!

She was there to learn so she decided not to allow any of Max's grumpiness to discourage her. She would do whatever task Max needed in the hope that her dream of becoming a better writer and one day becoming published, and best still, published by Max Moore, would eventually come true.

She also still struggled with her attraction to Max. Even though Max was mean and miserable, there was something about her authority that turned Rosa on. Aside from the other reasons Rosa was serving Max, she found herself wanting to do it, wanting to please Max, enjoying feeling intimidated by her.

The bubbling of the percolator snatched her out of her thoughts. She turned around to face the counter and poured the hot coffee into the mug. Max already stated that she liked her coffee black so she stirred it, placed it on a tray, and picked the tray up into her hands. She walked out of the kitchen, strolled through the hallway and into the office.

She opened the door with one hand and walked into the office, gently closing the door with her foot.

When she placed the coffee on Max's desk, Max reached her hand forward to receive the mug, their fingers brushed and Rosa paused as chills coursed through her veins. She felt shivers run all the way to between her legs and settle there.

"Thank you," Max said and raised the mug to her lips.

Rosa's cheeks were flushed, she turned around with her head dropped and walked back to her desk.

"I emailed you a manuscript, it was submitted by a writer for editing. Read it, it's brilliant and of industry-standard."

"Okay, ma'am."

"It's the first good thing I've read from a new writer in months!" she muttered under her breath.

Rosa lifted her eyes to regard her.

First good thing she's read in months from new writers! Ugh.

The words echoed in her head but she did not say anything, she couldn't.

Instead, she dropped her head and swiped her cursor to her mailbox.

"You could learn a thing or two from it."

"Yes, ma'am." She spoke without lifting her head.

"I meant that."

10

Rosa's days grew busier than ever. In the past, she had spent her daytime hours writing, working on her manuscripts at home, and in the late afternoon, she went to work at the restaurant to do her evening shift that lasted up until 10:30pm.

But for the past two weeks since she started working as Max's assistant, things had changed in her schedule.

She now woke up in the mornings and went for a run with Bailey. After which, she got back home to have some breakfast before taking a shower, dressing up, and driving to Pacific Heights to tend to Max and learn under her for six hours a day.

After working with Max, she would drive back to her neighborhood in Mission District and spend the next hours with Bailey before driving to the restaurant by 4pm to begin her evening shifts.

She could not tell if she was happy working as Max's assistant or if she was simply excited about the idea of being around her.

Max was blunt; blunt and hard, maybe too hard, and while something about that really attracted her to Max, it scared her just as much.

She had seen how Max treated writers, how she trashed manuscripts she didn't think worthy; she discarded them without a second thought. Yet she made Rosa type courteous emails explaining how sorry the company was to not be able to accept the writer's script at that time and some jargon about how the writer should try them again next time. Such emails always ended with, "If other opportunities arise in the company, we'll be happy to work with you."

And Rosa wondered if Max, who was actually WordFlux, meant any of it at all.

She sighed and closed the front door of the restaurant behind her. She climbed into her car, waving goodbye to Erin. She reversed into the street and accelerated down the road that led to her house.

It was 10:20pm and she didn't want to dwell on Max or on what it meant to be her assistant anymore, not that she could think of anything else.

But she would try.

She would really try, especially tonight when all she wanted to do was to get home, crawl into her bed, hold Bailey, and fall asleep.

MAX MOORE TOSSED in her bed, unable to sleep.

It was that bloody girl she'd let into her house, Rosa Martinez!

She was enjoying teaching her. But she couldn't stop thinking about teaching her other things.

Thoughts of her wouldn't let her be, reoccurring images flashing through her mind and Max burned between her thighs just thinking about her.

Fuck it! she swore, jumping up to her feet.

She strode to her high window and looked down into the street. It was quiet and partly deserted, except for some taxis driving past, a few nightcrawlers and lovers kissing under the night sky.

Not helping, she turned back around and walked to her bed. She dropped into the bed in a sitting position and snatched her phone from the bedside table.

She dialed Mary, a new girl she had been chatting with on Tinder.

"Hey," Mary spoke drowsily into the phone.

"Are you sleeping?"

"Just reading a book in bed. You okay?"

"Yeah, I just want to see you."

"Tonight?" Her voice was laced with excitement and curiosity.

"Yes, tonight."

"I thought we agreed to meet over the weekend?" She was obviously teasing and Max liked the tone of that.

"I couldn't wait."

"I'll be on my way. Text me your address."

Max texted her address and in less than an hour, Mary was knocking on her front door.

Diablo was barking at the door as Max climbed down the stairs.

She shushed the dog and shot a finger towards the stairs. "Go upstairs! Leave, Diablo!"

The dog dropped his head and whimpered away, disappearing into the house as opposed to climbing up the stairs as instructed.

Satisfied anyway, Max turned the doorknob and pulled the heavy wooden door open.

"Hi!" Mary smiled; she looked just like she did on her online profile.

Impressed, Max engulfed her into her arms and Mary chuckled excitedly. She pulled Mary in and kicked the door shut then pushed her back against the closed door. Already excited with anticipation and expectation, the young woman relaxed in

Max's arms and Max kissed her hard on the mouth.

They had talked about this, sexted long enough, and both women were ready.

Max tore Mary's shirt apart and Mary giggled in anticipation.

Max bent forward and took her breast into her mouth. She nibbled at her nipple and Mary moaned and slapped her hands to the wall behind for support. Max sucked her nipples interchangeably, running her tongue over the round skin of her breast down to her navel.

She trailed the girl's slender body with speedy, wet kisses, squeezing her small breasts and tugging at the nipples as she went.

She dropped to her knees and pushed the girl's short skirt up to her waist, and she smirked up at her as her clean shave glistened under Max's dim antechamber light. "Came ready, huh?"

"Ye-yeah," Mary replied shakily, clinging to the wall behind and looking down at Max in excited anticipation.

With her fingers, Max parted the lips of Mary's pussy and dove in with her tongue and her whole mouth focussing on Mary's pleasure.

Mary gasped and threw her head backward.

Max lifted Mary's right leg to rest on her shoulder, giving Max more room to work and she lost herself in Mary. It was a good way to stop thinking about Rosa.

"Ahh, ye-yes, yes," Mary groaned, grabbing onto Max's shoulders.

Max abruptly rose to her feet and pulled Mary by the hand to her front room. She gently but firmly pushed her against the table, but Mary peeled herself away from the table and kissed Max instead. She grabbed the top of Max's pajamas by the edges and pulled them over Max's head, exposing her breasts and muscular body and arms. Mary gushed, "You're so beautiful!" She kissed Max on the neck, licked her small breasts then slipped her fingers into the pants of Max's pajamas.

Mary pushed Max back onto the table and Max laid supine on the mahogany console table.

Mary dragged her pyjama pants completely down her legs and pushed her legs apart, then leaning forward on the edge of the table, she pushed her face into Max's pussy and Max moaned and grasped her blonde hair.

Mary steadied her tongue on Max's clitoris. She pushed two fingers inside Max then added a third finger and fucked her back and forth with her hot mouth still determinedly on Max's clitoris.

Max shut her eyes and pushed her hips up and down, hissing with pleasure.

She thought of Rosa, beautiful and tan with that smooth butter skin and a bright smile standing by her lawn in the sun, with the rays shining over her beautiful skin and her dark hair dancing gently across her shoulders... she imagined Rosa and her long coltish legs parted... Rosa and her big innocent eyes looking up at Max... she imagined ripping Rosa's flimsy summer dresses from her body... she imagined Rosa on her knees with Max's pleasure in her mouth...

Max groaned and stiffened against Mary's mouth and her body quaked in an explosive orgasm.

11

"Good morning Ms. Moore," Rosa greeted Max as she breezed into her home office the next morning.

"Good morning, Ms. Rosa, did you sleep well?"

Rosa paused in her tracks. She did a 360 and stood to stare wide-eyed at Max.

Max, who had been collecting books from the shelf, sensed Rosa's peering eyes so she looked over her shoulders and stared back at the smiling girl.

"What?" She shrugged briefly, darting her eyes around as if searching for what Rosa was staring at. "Is there a problem?"

Rosa looked pleased. "No, ma'am." She shook her head and her cheeks instantly flushed.

"So, are you going to tell me what it is?"

"You've never asked if I slept well before."

"Okay, well, I did today, now get to work!"

The smile disappeared from Rosa's lips. "Yes, ma'am." She bowed slightly and took her place at her desk.

"I received a script last night," Max began, moving away from the shelf to pace the floor. "Badly written! I got the message the writer was trying to portray, but the delivery of the narrative was off and it killed the entire story. So," she stopped to regard Rosa, "Your task today will be to rewrite that script. Make it engaging and realistic, and change the point of view from the third person to a first-person POV."

"Okay, ma'am." Rosa's fingers pressed the power button on her computer.

Max took her face in for a minute before walking back to her desk, to forward the soft copy of the manuscript to Rosa's mailbox.

Suddenly, Rosa jerked her head up and jumped from the chair. "I need to take Diablo for his walk."

"Don't worry about that today, Magda will take him; sit down."

"And your coffee?"

"I'll fetch my coffee myself."

Rosa's brow furrowed, confused, and Max read her expression and assured her, "It's fine, sit. I need the script in four days so get started already."

Rosa sat back down, pushed some hair behind her ear, and moved the mouse to her mailbox.

Rosa had a way about her every time she wrote, Max observed. Her long hair brushed against the surface of the desk and her full lips, parted, moved inaudibly, almost as if she was mouthing the words on the screen to herself. Her fingers, lean and tan and delicate, moved gracefully across the keyboard, creating swift tapping sounds as she punched at the keys.

Today, she wore a white shirt that buttoned up her neck, but the very top button betrayed her by coming undone.

Oblivious, Rosa continued working with her eyes fixed on the computer screen in front of her, and Max could not help but steal glances at her cleavage that the button had, unknowingly to Rosa, granted her a view.

Max swallowed hard and looked away to her computer, which like Rosa's, was sitting flipped open on her desk. But no matter how much she willed herself to focus on the screen in front of her, she found herself turning to steal glances at a busy Rosa.

She was so beautiful! As delicate as a butterfly, and Max wondered what her life was like.

It must have been the sense that everyone gets when someone is staring at them because suddenly Rosa whisked her head sideways. It happened so fast that Max didn't have time to look away and Rosa caught her, gazing at her, and even then, Max found herself unable to look away.

They held each other's gaze and Rosa smiled sweetly and returned her focus down to her work.

Max felt stupid.

What am I doing?

She rose from the desk and breezed out of the room, closing the door behind her. She marched into the guest bathroom, fixed her face under the tap, and turned the water on. The water ran sideways across her face, smearing her mascara. When she turned off the tap, she pinned her hands down on the sink and stared at her reflection looking back at her through the mirror.

What am I doing?

~

"Does she know?" inquired Isabella.

"*Nooo!*" Rosa dragged the word out.

"Oh my god, you have got it bad!" Isabella stated, and Rosa didn't say a word. "See? You can't even deny it."

"She's brilliant, Izzy, and what's more? She's powerful, she's strong, and her arms are so big she looks like she could pick me up and throw me over her shoulder. She's butch in the most beautiful way."

"But she's mean to you, you said that

many times in your text. I just don't get how you can be attracted to someone who won't cut you some slack."

"She excused me from walking Diablo and making her coffee today." Rosa shrugged a shoulder and scrunched her face as if her cousin could see her.

"Only because she needs you to finish working on that story."

"Yeah!" Rosa heaved and leaned back into her chair. "I don't know what's wrong with me." She bit her lower lip and rolled her eyes over the high ceiling. "She's way out of my league anyway and I'm so much younger than her. She would never take someone like me seriously."

"Exactly! Now you're thinking straight. You just nee—"

"Oh my God, she's coming back, I gotta go, bye!"

She placed the cellphone face down on the desk and sat with her shoulders high and fingers back on the keyboard.

Max pushed the door open and spoke as she walked to her desk, "Done with the first three chapters yet?"

Rosa was appalled by her question, but

she didn't show it. "No, ma'am. I'm only rounding up the first chapter."

Max turned and glared at her. "That's ridiculous! You should be past a chapter by now, it's been three hours."

"I'm taking my time; I wouldn't want to deliver a rushed work."

Max opened her mouth to say something but obviously restrained herself.

"I'm sorry, ma'am, I want to get it right for you," Rosa apologized.

She quickened her pace at the keyboard. Max nodded approvingly and left her to it.

BY 3PM, Rosa closed her computer and began to gather her things into her bag. She looked over at Max's seat, which was empty. She had *stepped out* is how she had put it and Rosa refused to concern herself with the details of her whereabouts.

Throwing the final item into her bag, she wore the handbag over her shoulder and walked out of the office into the front room. Diablo was standing in the entryway, whimpering with his tongue sticking out at her; a signal that usually indicated he was hungry.

"Hey!" Rosa dropped to her knees in front of the dog and smoothed a hand over his neck. She had been so engrossed in her work that she forgot to take the time to feed him and she had no idea how late Max would be back. She hadn't given any details. She sighed and looked down at her wrist; it was 3:15pm. She needed to be on her way already to be able to make it to the restaurant on time. Her shift started at 4pm. "Come on, boy!"

She rose to her feet and led the dog into the kitchen. The dog followed after her, panting hungrily.

Rosa reached up to the cabinet where the dog food was stacked, she felt her hand around the cupboard but it was empty.

Shoot!

She climbed down the stool and checked in the pantry, but there was no food there for Diablo either.

Oh no!

She stood back and lifted a palm to her head, weighing her options. Diablo was looking at her from the floor, barking hungrily.

She needed to be on her way already. One more glance at her watch confirmed she had 40 minutes left before she'd be late for her shift. The drive from Pacific Heights to the restaurant was exactly twenty-five minutes. If she left now, she'll make it just in time.

She glanced down at the barking dog and her heart melted at his brown eyes, they stared up at her, begging for her help.

"Come on!" she said and moved past the dog. The dog made a U-turn and ran after her. Together, they marched through the hallway and into the front room.

"You stay here, okay?" she said to the dog. "I'll be right back" The dog whimpered and sat down then Rosa pulled the door open and walked out of the house.

She stopped on the porch and contemplated whether to use her car or take a walk, shooting glances at the car then at the road. She quickly decided on the latter. The department store was right down the road, she could make a dash for it and be back in ten minutes.

Ten minutes? Nah!

She dipped into her bag for her car key, retrieved it, and double-clicked the tiny remote control before jumping into the Camry and starting the engine. She reversed into the road and was driving towards the department store within a minute.

When she pulled up into the parking area of the store, she saw that the lot was full. Hissing under her breath, she backed away and moved the car in circles, looking for a place to park. After spending about ten minutes moving around the line of cars, hoping someone would just drive out, she caught a customer walking out of the store with his hands full of groceries. She paused and watched where the aged man was headed, slowly following him at a distance.

When he got into one of the cars in the parking lot, Rosa accelerated her car to take a position that would enable her to swerve into line the moment the man moved his car out.

It was 3:48pm now.

The man sat in his car for a while and Rosa drummed her fingers impatiently against the steering wheel.

Eventually, the tires of the man's car began to move backward and Rosa cruised her car forward and took a sharp turn into the line the moment the man's car was fully vacated from the spot. She turned off the engine and jumped out of the car. She made a dash into the store and snatched some packets of dog food off the shelves.

Luckily for her, she didn't have to wait in a long line and in a few minutes, she was out of the store and racing to her car.

She arrived at the house and opened the door to a barking Diablo.

"Sorry boy," Rosa apologized as she shut the door behind her. "I could not find a place to park. Come here."

She breezed to the kitchen and found the dog plate, set it on the floor in front of Diablo, and emptied the pack of food into it. Diablo immediately rushed for the food, wagging his tail as he ate hastily.

She fetched his drinking bowl and stood by the sink. She turned on the tap and as she waited for the bowl to fill, she glanced down at her wristwatch again.

4:10pm.

The front door opened and Rosa heard giggles.

She turned off the water and placed the bowl down on the floor. Sounds of things clanking followed and Rosa lifted her head curiously. She paused, straining her ears to the confusing noise. Something clanged and then wild laughter rang into the air. Recognizing Max's voice, she sprung to her feet and walked out of the kitchen, tip-toeing her way through the hallway for no other reason than uncertainty.

She needed to get to work!

Her eyes widened at the sight before her eyes...

Max, bare-chested, was pressed to the wall by a girl whose face Rosa could not see because she was impatiently fighting with the button of Max's gray pants.

They were kissing and giggling, just like teenagers.

"Fuck!" Max swore and pushed the un-known woman away. She scrambled around confusingly for her blouse and the stranger finally noticed Rosa's presence. She exchanged confused yet unbothered glances between Max and Rosa.

Rosa paced, looking away awkwardly. Her heart raced and she wished the ground would just swallow her.

She had just seen her boss, naked, and with another woman...

Max finally found her blouse, she yanked it over her breasts and turned around to glare at Rosa. "What the fuck are you still doing at my house!"

"I-I'm so sorry," Rosa spoke with her head looking away as if she hadn't seen all there was to see already.

"You're not supposed to be here at this time!"

"I know, I-I'm so sorr—"

"Get out!" Max spat, pointing a finger towards the door and Rosa moved her feet.

She yanked the door open and heard Diablo emerge from behind her and start to bark. Without glancing backward, she pulled the door open and ran out into the yard.

She raced to her car, climbed into the vehicle, and wept over her steering wheel.

She couldn't explain why tears were streaming down her face, all she knew was that she felt upset and her heart was breaking into a thousand pieces.

12

The next morning, Rosa lay in her bed, not sure if she should go to work or not. Her puffy eyes, sore from last night's tears, watched Bailey; the dog was chewing on a squeaky ball at the foot of her bed, unaware of the raging emotions going on in her owner's mind.

She had hardly slept the night before. Images of Max and that woman kept flashing through her mind and it wouldn't stop hurting. Still, as awkward as it had felt, *still felt*, to see her icon of a boss in nothing but her work pants, she couldn't stop thinking about Max's tight abs and the way the muscles were so finely defined. Max's small breasts and the small hard nipples. Max's strong muscular shoulders.

Rosa tossed.

Focus!

She should not be thinking about Max and her tough arms, worse, imagining her nipples in Rosa's mouth.

She hadn't shown up at the restaurant yesterday either; what she needed to do was to come up with something, any reasonable excuse that would justify her absence from work, then call Mr. Pablo and see if he would buy it. Or better yet, go into the restaurant to provide her explanation and apology in person.

I'll think of what to say in the shower.

Satisfied with her decision, she climbed out of the bed and walked into her bathroom.

∼

"Is she here yet?" Max's eyes were looking out the window of her home office.

"No, ma'am," replied Magda. "Can I get you anything?" she asked with her gloved hands holding on to the mop stick, dipped in the half-full bucket of water.

"No," Max swallowed. She swept the blind closed and looked briefly over her shoulders at the housekeeper. "Go back to work, Magda." She took two steps towards her desk then stopped in her tracks.

"Hey, Magda!" she called out to the woman who had almost disappeared behind the door.

"Yes?" she retraced backward.

"Can you please dash to the mall to refill Diablo's food? He was out yesterday morning."

"There's food in the pantry for Diablo, ma'am."

"That's not possible; there was none by the time I stepped out yesterday afternoon, and I didn't buy any."

Magda cocked her head. "I don't know how, but the pantry is full with his food, including treats," Magda said, and Max's jaw dropped. "It must be the girl, Rosa, she loves the dog." she concluded.

Max swallowed hard. "T-that's fine," she stammered. "Thank you."

Magda nodded and walked away into

the hallway.

She had to pin her hand down to her desk to keep herself from staggering.

Her heart raced, overwhelmed with un-explained emotions.

At first, she had tossed restlessly in her bed last night, consumed with guilt over how she rudely yelled at Rosa the after-noon before. After Rosa had left, Max had felt so disoriented that she sent the other woman home, took a large vodka with coca cola, and withdrew into her room. She thought the vodka would send her into a long night of sleep, but she had been asleep for barely four hours before her unsettled heart jolted her awake. Now, she was finding out that Rosa had been to the store to get Diablo's food and that was why she was still at Max's house when she returned.

She sank down into the chair, unable to contain herself.

What was happening to me? she thought to herself.

Ever since that woman came to work under her, she had fought emotions she didn't even know she had, drowning it all in vodka and casual sex; it was the life she had plunged herself into since Caroline, yet, somehow, when Rosa showed up, that life-style suddenly felt wrong and she wasn't sure if that was a good thing or a bad thing. And as if the exciting uneasiness Rosa created in her was not enough, she had warmed up to Diablo pretty fast. Max hadn't expected such a bond between the two, at least, not so fast yet, she had caught them on different occasions playing, and that in itself sent warmth through her heart, and now, now the girl had gone out, on her own, and from her own pocket, bought food for Diablo and all she got in return was a yell, a horrifying yell.

Max's heart sunk.

This is too much, she thought.

This was too much for her to handle. These emotions were more than she could bear.

She pushed her hands on the kitchen sink and dropped her head forward, panting softly. She was so destabilized that she didn't hear Magda walk in, and the poor woman had to repeat herself.

"Excuse me, ma'am!" And this time, Max yanked her head up. "Is everything okay?" Magda was concerned but remained situated at the doorway.

"Yes!" Max spat, irritated more by her own emotions than the older woman's innocent concerns. "What is it?"

"Rosa, she's here."

Her eyes widened. "What?"

It was more of a murmur but the older woman heard it. Satisfied that she had delivered her message, she bobbed her head then walked away.

Max pushed away from the sink and turned around, then turned back around, confused.

Calm down, just calm down.

She grabbed her cup and turned on the faucet. Full, she lifted the cup to her mouth and emptied the water in one hasty gulp. She jammed the cup down on the counter and straightened the hem of her pants with her hands. She took a deep breath, counted to ten then exhaled.

Finally feeling like she had control, she heaved one last time and shot her eyes towards the door.

∾

Rosa's mind had been made up. She had exited the bathroom into her bedroom, changed into her sportswear, and stepped out of her apartment. Bailey immediately hopped after her.

"Come on," she had beckoned to the dog, and the both of them picked up the pace and sank speedy feet onto the pavement of the quiet street.

As they took a turn at the end of Balmy street, Rosa's phone beeped.

She pressed a finger to her Air pods with her feet still racing. "Hello?"

"Hi, sis!"

Her feet screeched to a halt. "Thank God you called."

"Why? What happened?"

"Cut the excitement, Lola!"

Lola laughed, "Well, you sound like you're about to say something fun!"

"I walked in on Max."

"Okay? Doing what?"

"Topless! She was—"

"You know you can actually say the word right? It's called *naked*."

"Whatever, Lola- she wasn't totally naked anyway... just, you know, top half!"

Lola guffawed.

"I'm not sure I can go back there—"

"No, Rosa, no! Don't do that." And Rosa imagined her sister leaning forward on her office desk and jamming a finger in the air. "You wanted this, you wanted this so bad."

Rosa combed her fingers through her hair. She heaved and lowered herself down on an old trunk of a fallen tree. "I don't know. I don't know how to face her again."

"You just do," Lola insisted. "Go back there, do what you must but don't quit until you've got your book published. You've come too far to back down now."

"Wow, easy, Lola, you sound like Mom."

"Well."

"Are you biting on a fruit? I can hear crunching."

"It's an apple. I fucking hate it when my boss calls me out in front of everyone!"

"And an apple would fix that?" Rosa scrunched her face.

"Don't worry about me, Rosa, just go back to Max!"

"Yeah, well, thanks. I guess?"

"You're welcome!"

13

Rosa arrived at Max's and headed straight through to the office, darting glances between her chair and that of Max's. Both were empty.

She should sit down, but she couldn't. She couldn't, *not this way...*

"You're late," a voice called from behind her, and she whisked around to see Max standing by the doorway. She wore light gray pants with a tight black button down shirt and Rosa loved how good she looked.

"I'm sorry," Rosa said, trying not to swoon too obviously.

"Stop saying that," Max dismissed calmly with a flap of the hand. She closed the door and began to stroll towards her desk. "You always say that," she concluded.

Rosa watched her, unsure whether to continue or to stop. Quickly deciding, she waited for her to sit down on her big chair then she continued, "I'm really sorry about yesterday—"

"No," Max stopped her before she could finish. "I should be the one apologizing. I am sorry."

Rosa's eyes widened.

Did Max Moore just give me an apology?

She recovered quickly, she had to, before Max read her expression and said something, anything, to wither down the effect of her apology, and whatever was causing her to be unusually soft to her that morning.

So, Rosa twiddled with her fingers instead, nervously.

Max Moore just apologized to me, wow!

"You shouldn't have had to see that, and I'm sorry I yelled at you."

"It's fine." Rosa dropped her head. Her fingers quivered and she pushed strands of dark hair behind her ears.

"No, really, it isn't," Max insisted and rose from her desk.

She walked around her table to stand before Rosa and Rosa lifted her head and caught the older woman's gaze.

Her heart skipped.

Max's eyes were a deep dark green, she noticed. They sometimes looked so dark they were almost black, but here in the light she could see they were the darkest green, like a forest, and they held the calmest sincerity and tenderness she could imagine. Max was standing so close, tall and strong, and Rosa inhaled her scent, freshly bathed, with an overwhelming woody fragrance.

Rosa dropped her head.

"Thank you for Diablo's food, you didn't have to," Max said, and Rosa could not lift her head nor offer a reply. She burnt, fiery on the inside, and it was so hot that she could not find her voice.

She wanted to say, *It was nothing*, or *Thank you*, but she couldn't.

Max put a finger under her chin and slowly raised her head to look at her, and Rosa gasped.

Max was so imposing and beautiful, and as Rosa gazed up at her, it felt like Max could protect her. Like she could fight for her, like she could—

The downward movement of Max's head stopped her thoughts, it stopped time, and Rosa could only freeze and watch Max lower her face down unto hers. Rosa's lips parted instinctively...

The sharp sound of something smashing caused Max to jump backward and so did Rosa.

Max looked towards the door and marched heavily to pull the door open. She walked through the doorway and closed the door behind her. "Magda?" Rosa could hear her calling. "What was that?"

"WHAT HAPPENED?" Max was asking Magda, standing over the hunched woman in the living room. She was gathering broken pieces of marble from the floor with Diablo barking on incessantly. "Is that the dog sculpture I got on my trip to Japan?" Max was appalled.

The older woman lifted her head. "I'm so sorry, ma'am."

"How did you knock that over?"

"I was—"

"How could you be so clumsy, Magda?"

"I'm so sorry. You can deduct the money for the sculpture from my salary."

"No, I wouldn't do that. It would mean depriving you of your pay for months." Max sighed and lifted a palm to her brow. "You scared me."

"I'm so sorry, ma'am."

"It's ok. I'm sorry, I'm not mad. Just clean this up," Max said and turned around to walk back towards her office.

"Thank you," Magda called after her.

Max walked to her office and stopped when she reached the door.

Memories of the moment before the interruption came rushing back to her, and she stared at the doorknob, nervous to touch the handle and open the door.

She didn't know how it had happened; seeing Rosa that morning all long legs in the little skirt had intensified all the emotions she had been feeling...

Rosa was so beautiful, so tender, and as delicate as a flower. Feminine and sweet, she was everything Max was not. That opposite nature of hers; innocent and awkward, attracted Max so much, she could almost not help herself any longer. She didn't even know for sure if Rosa was into women yet she had found herself almost kissing her...

Magda's footsteps approached the hallway and Max heaved and grabbed the knob of the door. She turned it open and pushed the wooden door ajar. Rosa was sitting at her desk now, with hands typing at her keyboard. Her eyes were focused on the computer screen as if the moment they had didn't just happen, but Max knew better, she was too old to be fooled.

Letting things be, she shut the door behind her and walked over to her desk. She sat down in her chair and adjusted her MacBook on top of her work desk.

"Hey," she said, and Rosa lifted her brown eyes to regard her face, "How far have you gone with the script?"

"I'm on the fourth chapter, ma'am."

"You don't have to keep calling me that,"

she said, and Rosa's cheeks flushed. "Simply call me Max, okay?"

"Okay, ma... sorry, I meant, Max."

Max smiled. "Email me the pages you've worked on so far, will you?"

"Yes, ma—Max."

"It will take some getting used to, don't worry."

Rosa smiled.

She returned her attention to her laptop and scrolled to her mailbox. She double-clicked on Max's name, it had threaded messages of their previous conversations, all of which were business related. She attached a copy of the three chapters she had edited and clicked send.

"Thank you," Max said, "Received."

Rosa nodded.

"Hurry up on the next chapters, okay?"

"Okay."

Oh god, I can't stop thinking about kissing her.

Willing herself to concentrate, she shifted her eyes from Rosa and fixed them on the screen in front of her.

Hours ticked past and Rosa stood from her chair. "May I be excused?" she asked.

"Sure," Max responded with eyes focused on her computer.

"Thank you," Rosa said. She grabbed her phone and stepped away from her desk. She pulled the closed door open and stepped out into the hallway. Diablo was sleeping on the bottom of the U-shaped stairs.

"Hi, Magda," she said as she sighted Magda emerging from one of the rooms. She had changed from the housekeeping uniform to her own clothes and was wearing her bag over her shoulders. "Done for the day?"

Magda smiled, "Yes, child. Is Ms. Moore in?" she pointed towards the office door.

"Yeah," Rosa replied sweetly. When Magda made the turn towards the office, Rosa walked to the stairs and sat beside Diablo. The big dog cooed in his sleep and snuggled up to Rosa. Rosa allowed the dog to drop his head on her thighs then proceeded to rub his neck.

As her hands stroked Diablo, her thoughts drifted to the work she had just submitted to Max. She had given it her best shot. After learning Max's writing style for weeks now, she applied every lesson she picked from reading her style of preference and every correction Max gave over any work, including the snarky comments she made. Still, she was nervous and questioned if her efforts would be good enough.

So far, Max had not been easy to please, she switched on and off like a light switch; one minute she was nice and kind and the next, her grumbling nature returned. It was like something was eating her on the inside, something so strong that it held her back from being the tender and accommodating person Rosa knew she could be. Something must have happened to make her this way, and often Rosa wondered what that something could be.

"Bye, Ms. Rosa!" Magda's voice rang into her thoughts.

"See you later, Magda!" she replied and watched the older woman walk through the anteroom to the front door. She stopped at the console in the entryway and wiped her fingers over something sitting on the top of the console, something Rosa could not see but imagined to be some particles of dust. Done, the older woman proceeded to pull the door open and walked out into the foggy afternoon. Then she released the door to shut behind her.

Rosa looked down at Diablo, who was now awake and sitting quietly with her, and scratched the dog's neck. "Let's hope your mama likes my work."

She rose from the stairs, took two steps down, and walked back to the office.

She pulled the door open and glanced briefly at Max; she still had her eyes on the computer with her black framed glasses on. Rosa liked those glasses, especially because they matched Max's short dark hair. And she liked how they sat on her square face— very elegant and serious.

She moved away from the door and began to stroll towards her desk. She walked around the L-shaped desk and swiped her hands behind her dress as she sat down.

Max sighed. She peeled her glasses away from her face and leaned back into her chair. She lifted her eyes to regard Rosa and their eyes met.

"I like it," Max said, and Rosa flushed happily. "I like it, you got the flow and grammar just as I wanted and it is so much better in the 1st person POV. You have given it a strong voice. Good job."

"Thank you," Rosa could almost not contain herself.

"Finish up with the remaining chapters, I have another assignment for you. This time, I'll teach you how to write in the third-person multiple, but focus on the chapters you have left for now. You did well!"

"That means so much to me, ma'am." Rosa couldn't believe she was actually getting praise finally from the enigmatic and hard to please Max Moore.

"Max," Max corrected her.

"Thank you, thank you *sooo* much"

"Good girl." Max looked her directly in the eye. That forest green gaze glared with intensity.

Rosa felt pleasure rush right through her body and settle between her legs.

Max glanced down at her wristwatch and rose from the chair. "I have a meeting for 2pm at WordFlux. I may be gone for a while."

And it saddened Rosa that she would be left alone in the office, without her.

"Lock up when you have to leave, okay?"

"Okay."

Max grabbed her cellphone and walked around her large desk to the bookshelf to collect a file. Rosa was stealing glances at her. Max moved between a few files on the shelf before pulling the folder that contained the documents she wanted. She flipped the large file open, perused through its contents, and closed it back, satisfied.

Rosa rose to her feet. She couldn't hold it back any longer, another second would be too long a time. Like a zombie, she stood still on her feet, staring at Max. As the woman was about to step away from the shelf, her eyes lifted and she caught Rosa's gaze staring at her with her chest rising and dropping behind her blouse. When Max spotted her hands, tightening into a fist on her sides, her brows flinched inquisitively and she shifted her eyes up to Rosa's face. "Are you okay?"

Rosa charged towards her, shocked by her own bravery. She stopped when she was standing in front of Max, and her body shook, dizzy with desire. Daringly, she craned her neck upwards and Max dropped the contents of her hands to the floor. She grabbed Rosa, pulled her in, and sent her mouth crashing down on hers.

Rosa moaned into Max's kiss.

She wrapped her arms around Max's neck and the woman edged her backward until she was pressed against the tall bookshelf. Books fell to the ground, decorative ornaments crashed to the floor, but they didn't care. This had been a long time coming. This electrifying tension had built up for too long between them and now they burned in each other's mouths. Rosa thought she would drown in this stream of ecstasy that Max's mouth was sending through her. Finally, she could touch her. Finally, she could feel Max's buff body pressing into her, Max's hard thigh pressed between her legs and Rosa felt a hot wet heat of desire flooding her.

Max grabbed Rosa's left breast through her dress; she squeezed the full softness and Rosa felt electricity running through her. She kissed Rosa's even harder and Rosa felt devoured by her. Using both hands, Max tore the fabric of Rosa's blouse and broke away from her mouth to look at her.

"You're not wearing a bra," she observed excitedly.

Rosa was flushed and excited to feel Max's gaze on her breasts. Max's eyes were hungry.

"Ah, I um usually don't, my boobs are just small and they don't really move," Rosa mumbled.

"You're perfect." Max breathed.

Rosa felt suddenly awkward yet still so excited by Max's eyes on her body. Max seemed to sense it and grabbed Rosa's neck to pull them close again. She ran her fingers up into Rosa's hair, inhaling deeply and Rosa hoped that the scent of her shampoo was still there. "I want to fuck you so badly," she groaned into her hair and Rosa shook, feverish with desire. Warm fluid escaped down her upper thigh and she knew that it would take just one touch *there* from Max to completely send her over the edge.

Max swept Rosa up into her arms and carried her to her desk. Being lifted up and held by Max's strong arms was everything she had imagined. Max placed Rosa on her desk and ripped her shirt and skirt completely off her body. She picked the sides of Rosa's panties and Rosa squirmed suddenly uncomfortably naked as Max pulled them roughly down her legs.

"God!" Max gasped, taking in Rosa's naked body and soaking wet panties on the floor. Rosa squirmed on the desk, trying and failing to avoid her gaze.

Max ran her hands over Rosa's body and Rosa felt like she was on fire. Bolts of electricity shot through her from Max's hands.

Max tweaked her nipples with her fingers, rubbing them in circles between her fingers and pulling on Rosa's erect nipples. "So full and soft," she groaned, as Rosa yelped. The pulling almost hurt her. It trod the fine line between pleasure and pain and Rosa found herself liking it.

"You like me pulling on them?"

Rosa moaned and looked away. Max stopped pulling on them and Rosa felt suddenly dismayed that she wasn't feeling that intensity anymore.

"Um.. yes... it hurts.. but like good hurt."

"Good girl, baby."

Max's fingers pulled at her nipples some more and Rosa felt like she was so close to orgasming from this alone. She had never considered her nipples a particular point of pleasure for her. But then, nobody had ever pulled them roughly like Max was doing and she had never desired someone as much as she desired Max.

Max replaced her fingers with her mouth on Rosa's right nipple. Sucking hard, biting, both at her nipple and at her breast. Rosa moaned loudly and felt suddenly very not in control of her own body. Her fingers ran through Max's short hair.

"O-oh!" she cried as Max sucked her breast, slowly at first and then, all at once. Max moved between her breasts, sucking and grabbing and kneading and pulling her nipples.

Rosa felt a hot hot heat building inside of her. She opened her legs and adjusted her hips slightly finding Max's pelvis tight against her clit. Rosa's orgasm sliced through her seconds later right through her body and she found herself screaming. She felt hot liquid gush down her inner thighs. She didn't recognise herself. *Who was this person who came screaming from having her nipples pulled and sucked hard?*

As she recovered Max was smiling at her. She gathered a limp Rosa up in her arms again and lifted her off the desk. "Let's go to my bedroom," she said, "I want to have all of you."

Rosa leaned upward and kissed Max passionately. Max moved with Rosa in her arms, out of her office, and into the hallway, kissing.

Rosa's lips wouldn't let go, her hands were around Max's neck, and she continued to kiss the Max as she climbed the stairs with Rosa in her arms.

Finally, they reached the top of the stairs and Max kicked her bedroom door open, stepped in, and kicked it back closed. She moved to the big bed and dropped Rosa into it. Rosa felt exposed again but she liked it more this time. Stepping back, with her eyes fixed on Rosa's naked body, Max peeled herself out of her suit until she was standing naked. Her body was so firm and strong and muscular. Rosa couldn't stop watching her. The fine muscles of her legs. The dark thatch of hair between her legs. The strong upper body that had just carried her.

Rosa inhaled in excitement.

Max climbed into the bed from the foot of the mattress and knelt at Rosa's feet.

"Spread your legs for me," she commanded.

Rosa obeyed straight away even though she felt exposed. The thrill of it ran through her. "I want to touch you," Rosa mumbled, knowing it wasn't her place to talk.

"You are touching me," Max said as her eyes lingered between Rosa's thighs and Rosa felt the heat of her gaze. "You are touching me more than you can imagine."

Max moved between Rosa's legs and Rosa felt her fingers suddenly sliding through the slick wetness between her legs and spreading her lips apart. "Oh god..." Rosa gasped.

Max studied her pussy with her eyes and fingers as she slid her fingers around teasing her and opening her up. Rosa closed her eyes. Nothing like this had ever

happened to her before. She felt so embarrassed but so utterly turned on. It felt so
good. She felt that hot hot heat beginning
to build deep inside her again.

"You look so fucking beautiful, Rosa.
Every inch of you. Inside and out. I want to
study every single part of your body and
pleasure every part of you with my fingers
and my tongue."

She rubbed Rosa's parted lips then her
clitoris, and Rosa arched her back and bit
her teeth on the back of her wrist.

Max played with her pussy, sending
strokes down and up her wetness and rubbing her excitedly. Rosa closed her eyes and
moaned and sucked on the back of her
wrist. All she could think of was what Max
was doing to her body. Max dipped a finger
slowly inside her and pulled it out again to
roll in circles around her opening. Rosa
could feel herself dripping with wetness,
and Max's finger glided smoothly against
her slickness.

She arched her back and moaned softly.
She wanted more. She craved Max deep inside her. She needed to feel her properly

inside her so deeply. Max, however, was in no rush.

Max wrapped her arms around Rosa's thighs and pulled her further down to her mouth. She kissed her pussy and sent her tongue between her thick lips. Rosa gasped loudly. She saw her own bite marks on her wrist.

Rosa lost herself in the exquisite feeling of Max's mouth and tongue. She had no doubt she was in the hands of an expert. She sucked Rosa's whole clit into her mouth, then her labia, taking it in turns, sucking each one into her mouth deeply. She licked in upward strokes right up from bottom to top of her pussy. Rosa moaned further. She felt Max's tongue push into her and she felt her own hips pushing up onto Max's tongue. Then Max took hold under Rosa's thighs and pushed her legs up and back until they were folded up against her stomach and her feet were up in the air. Then she felt Max's tongue once again, hot and wet on her anus. She was shocked and tensed momentarily, but it felt so beautiful and Max seemed so into it. Rosa found herself relaxing into Max's tongue on her asshole. Max's mouth kissing her asshole and both sides of the cleft of her ass. Max's tongue running pointedly around the rim. Then... *Oh god..* Max's tongue pushing slightly inside of her. Rosa moaned loudly. Max moved into bold sweeps of her tongue from Rosa's ass right up to her clit. Rosa felt her orgasm building inside of her as Max's tongue pressed firmly against her.

She felt her grip tighten in Max's hair, and she came hard in Max's mouth screaming again.

Max moved up her body to her face. Rosa saw the juice of her own orgasm all over Max's face and for a moment was embarrassed.

Then Max kissed her mouth deeply and Rosa tasted herself. Tasting her sex mingled with Max tasted so perfect. She licked tentatively and gently around Max's mouth and chin cleaning her orgasm from Max's beautiful face. Max moved her face to allow her to clean it. She reached to touch Max's breast and Max grabbed her hands and pinned them down to the bed.

"Why can't I touch you?" she asked, eyes dark with desire, and Max stood up from the bed. She walked to her drawer and removed a set of black handcuffs and Rosa felt her eyes widen.

Max walked back to the bed and raised her eyes to a point above Rosa's head. Rosa didn't even think twice- her hands automatically moved above her head in submission. Max cuffed them to the head of the bed and returned to lie next to Rosa. Rosa was in a world lost in time; she couldn't believe this was happening, *to her,* nothing could ever top this experience, and she never wanted this to end. Max was an absolute *god,* and in her presence she wanted to dwell forever. She was feeling sensations she never had before. Max could do with her body as she pleased.

Max's mouth found Rosa's breasts again and she caressed one with her hand and sucked on the other with her mouth. She pulled on Rosa's nipple again which was so sensitive now and Rosa nearly came again right there.

Max pulled and sucked, slapped and bit, and Rosa could only moan in ecstasy. How had she never known what incredible pleasure being rough with her breasts and nipples would bring her? When Max's fingers began to glide down her chest, past her abdomen, and down in between her thighs, Rosa's legs were wide apart and ready. With Max's mouth glued to her breasts, her fingers found her in circular motions and Rosa arched her hips forward, desperate yet again to feel Max deep inside her.

Max caressed her swollen clit with her fingers, groaning against her breasts as her fingers slipped around her warm slippery heat. She was sucking on her nipple while her fingers played between Rosa's legs.

Suddenly Rosa felt a finger push firmly inside her and she gasped.

"Do you want to feel me inside you, baby?" Max murmured.

"Um.." Rosa felt Max's finger curling against her G spot. "Oh god, yes. More than anything. Please."

Suddenly she felt another finger join the first and it felt amazing. She opened her legs wider. She wanted Max to take her in every way possible. "Ye-yes!" she cried.

Max began to fuck her with her fingers hard and deep. Suddenly Rosa wasn't sure how many fingers, only that she was wide open and wet and wanting and felt like she could take anything. Max's mouth sucked at her sore nipple and Rosa arched her body, restrained by the handcuffs. She liked how they bit into her skin when she tried to move. Max pulled her fingers upward to rub at her clit before plunging them back inside her to push in and out. When she steadied her fingers inside of her and curved them upwards, stroking steadily, Rosa felt the sensation rush from the toes of her feet to the walls of her vagina. She arched her body upwards and stiffened as she felt the quake of an almighty orgasm erupt through her and she cried out loudly. Then she fell limply back on the bed.

Rosa lay dazed with her eyes closed for what felt like minutes but was probably only seconds. She was lost in pleasure. She suddenly felt Max's fingers at her mouth pushing inside her parted lips, and Rosa sucked on them automatically, staring into Max's green eyes.

"Clean these, baby. Good girl." Max said as Rosa suckled happily tasting her own pussy on Max's strong thick fingers.

I love her! Rosa thought helplessly.

As Max finally withdrew her fingers from Rosa's mouth she felt suddenly empty. "Can I touch you now?" Rosa's words were more of a plea than a request. "Please."

Max leaned across her and reached to the bedside drawer. She pulled the top drawer open and felt her hands around for the keys. Once she touched them, she picked them out and stretched upward to loosen the cuffs around Rosa's hands. She carefully pulled Rosa's hands from the cuffs and Rosa saw the red welts around her wrists as she lowered her hands. She was partly shocked. But she liked them. She found herself marvelling at the marks they had left. The marks Max had left on her body. She smiled to herself and Max kissed the marks.

Rosa ran her newly free arms around Max in a hug. She kissed her lips and ran her delicate fingers down Max's buff arms. "You're so strong," she moaned, kissing her arms, from her shoulders all the way down to the tips of her fingers. Then she sucked Max's fingers into her mouth again.

She moved her body against Max, and Max allowed her to roll over on top of her.

With their lips glued, Rosa continued to twirl her tongue against Max's, exchanging heat and the sweet sensation that kisses bring.

She writhed on top of her, their bodies were pressing and breasts rubbing; she could not get enough of Max's body. She had worshipped this woman, adored her for so long that now that she was in her bed, now that she had Max's arms around her, she never wanted to let go. Nothing mattered anymore, nothing else mattered at all.

Time froze for Rosa; the world could come to an end around them and she wouldn't care. She was with Max, naked, together.

She touched small Max's breasts and kissed the soft flesh. She didn't have the precision that Max did but she felt satisfied just being able to touch her at all. Rosa moved down Max's big body and rested between her thick thighs. She smelled the sweet sharp scent of her sex.

She smells so good.

Rosa put her lips to the thick dark hair

between Max's legs and kissed her warm heat tentatively.

Max had no such patience and grabbed a handful of her hair pressing Rosa's face deep between her legs.

"When you pleasure me, I need you to mean it. I need your mouth on me like I am your last meal. Understand?"

Rosa tried to nod her head but it was trapped between Max's hand in her hair and her pussy in her face.

"Good girl."

Rosa sent her tongue immediately between Max's hot swollen lips. She could barely breathe as she licked and sucked and used her mouth and tongue as though she was making out with Max's pussy. She felt Max's hand tighten in her hair and Max began to grind into her face. Her nose, her chin, her mouth. Max was using them all to take her pleasure. Rosa shut her eyes and swallowed the moisture spilling from Max's pussy as her tongue continued to work hard. She gasped breaths where she could. Max was beginning to groan loudly.

Max took in a sharp breath. "Push your fingers into me,"

Rosa moved her mouth to Max's clit and pushed two fingers inside of her gently. "Four fingers. And fuck me. Hard. Like you mean it. Keep your mouth on my clit." she commanded, and Rosa obeyed.

Max arched her back as Rosa pushed into her with four fingers. It was tight but Max was so very wet and so open to her that Rosa surprised herself with the ease at which she could get inside Max. She began to fuck Max as hard as she could and Max rode her fingers.

"Add your thumb, baby. I want to feel your whole hand in me."

Rosa obeyed immediately although it wasn't something she had done before. She folded her thumb into her hand and pushed into Max. It caught at her knuckles the widest part and Rosa stopped.

"Keep the pressure on, good girl." Rosa pushed harder and she saw Max wince but at the same time push down onto her hand and suddenly she was deep inside. with her whole hand. She looked down and saw Max's pussy close tight around her wrist. Her whole hand was inside.

"Now move your fingers slowly and carefully and close them into a fist shape."

It wasn't easy but Rosa adjusted her fingers inside and smiled to herself.

Max's hand pushed Rosa's mouth back onto her clit. She moaned loudly and moved herself on Rosa's hand.

Max's hips rocked faster, and her grip grew firmer on Rosa's hair. "Keep at it, *yeah, just like that, baby…*"

Rosa felt Max's body tighten.

An orgasm built through her and she erupted, jerking convulsively against Rosa's face.

Max let out a loud breath and relaxed onto the bed. Rosa crawled up the bed and settled at Max's side. She slipped her leg between Max's thighs and glided her arm around Max's waist, then she rested her head on her chest. Max welcomed her snuggle with both her arms, she locked them around Rosa, and wordlessly, with nothing but the sound of the ticking clock on the wall between them, they drifted off to sleep; slowly at first, and then, all at once.

14

The weights felt heavy as Max worked through the reps of her lower body routine. The bar was across her shoulders as she squatted. Sweat glistering down her face and arms. She couldn't stop thinking about Rosa.

Yesterday was amazing—it was beyond amazing! She hadn't known for sure that Rosa had felt the things she felt all those weeks, but now she knew for sure. Rosa wanted her so much. Rosa's body had responded in every way possible to her. Max could hardly believe it when Rosa had kissed her.

Yet, too pleased to waste a second pondering or weighing the consequences of her assistant making a move on her, too full with weeks of built-up passion and sleepless nights; wondering what she would taste like, and feel like under her, she damned all defenses and welcomed her advances and as novice-like as her strokes were, Max enjoyed every moment with her. Rosa was so beautiful, so soft, so delicate, way beyond what she had even imagined. Her body had opened to Max like a beautiful flower and Max had loved every second of it.

Max returned the barbell to the rack.

Just reminiscing about last evening made Max moist between her thighs; it made her want to dash up the stairs, spread Rosa's thighs and do it all over again.

She climbed the stairs out of the basement and appeared in the hallway. Magda was off today, she thought to herself as she walked down the quiet hallway. She took the stairs that led up to the upper portion of her house then took a turn into her bedroom. Rosa was still sleeping, curved on the bed like a living doll, her dark hair was sprawled out across the pillow and she looked peaceful, so peaceful and at ease and Max could not resist the instinctive smile that ran across her lips.

Rosa was drop-dead gorgeous, and last night beat her imagination—and previous experiences—still, this was not right and she could not ignore that sting of guilt that tugged at her heart.

Max shook her head to shake away the thoughts. She turned around and headed towards her bathroom. There were so many things she wanted to do to Rosa, so many, including keeping her safe and being there for her in every way.

Max showered and dressed and headed down to the office. She picked up her phone and the screen showed several missed calls, mostly from the office. She had abandoned her phone downstairs in the heat of passion, too lost in Rosa to even call the office and excuse herself from the planned meeting.

God I don't know the last time I was this unprofessional!

Hissing under her breath, she dialed Kimberly.

"Oh, thank goodness!" Kimberly exclaimed as soon as she picked the call. "We were worried about you."

"I know, I'm sorry," Max apologized.

"It's unlike you not to show up."

"I know, I got distracted. How did it go?"

"I handled it. We reiterated the minutes of the last meeting and brushed through the topic for yesterday, only briefly, though, as I knew you would rather chair the meeting yourself."

"Good. Please reschedule for this afternoon and send an apology to all attendees, I will be there unfailingly today."

Max's eyes lifted to Rosa walking through the door, fully dressed with a smile across her lips.

"Right," she spoke into the phone, shifting her eyes away from Rosa. "Yes, I'll be there, definitely. Thank you." She moved the phone away from her ear and ended the call.

"Hey," Rosa greeted.

"You're awake," Max stated.

"Yeah," Rosa said sounding panicked, "I slept like a log, but I need to go. My dog, Bailey. She has been on her own overnight. I know my neighbor popped in on after lunch and took her out for a little walk. She has done that every day I am here, and she will have had food and water, and she probably won't have cared much, she is such an independent soul, but oh god, I am such a bad dog mom."

Max looked shocked, "Of course. Do you need help?"

She watched Rosa, lowering down to sit at her desk. "I need my phone and my bag. Ah here is my phone," she retrieved it from the desk, glancing at Max as she picked up the device. Her screen unlocked to her face and almost immediately, her smile metamorphosed into a frown. "Oh my god! Mr. Pablo!" And she jumped up from her chair.

"Who's that?"

"He's my manager, at the restaurant where I work."

"Oh!"

"He's going to kill me!" Rosa complained worriedly. "I've missed work for two nights!"

Max wanted to ask why, then she remembered last night, and the night before, and her stomach churned.

"He's really strict, if you don't show up

for three shifts in a row, you'll lose your job."

"Go, please. Let me know if I can do anything to help. And don't worry about work today.. you don't need to do anything here. It can wait."

"Thank you, thank you so much!" She was jittery. She gathered her phone and computer into her bag.

She dashed over to Max's desk, leaned over, and attempted to kiss her. Max dodged the kiss.

Rosa paused, eyes widening. With her hands still on her desk, she gazed at Max, confused.

"Last night shouldn't have happened." Max's words were calm and she watched Rosa's eyes moisten.

It hurt so badly saying the words, and she wanted to stop talking. To reach up and wipe her tears, to let Rosa kiss her, to do more than let her kiss her, but she couldn't, she *wanted* to, but she just could not.

"I'm sorry."

Rosa's broken face sent daggers through her heart; it broke her to be *breaking* her, and unlike the other girls in the past, Rosa was not lashing words at her. Instead, she was frozen to her spot for a second. Rosa stared at her silently and the tears jumped down her eyes to her cheeks.

"I'm so sorry, Rosa. I've been unprofessional. I have taken advantage of my position as your boss, your teacher, your mentor." Max was unable to fight the feelings of guilt that had haunted her the moment she woke up and found Rosa sleeping away in her arms. The woman was so much younger, her assistant, working under her, her student and in her home. Rosa had said she would do anything and Max had taken advantage of that. It was so unprofessional of her. She had taken advantage of everything about the situation. It's all she could think about, it was all she could feel behind that burn that itched for her.

Rosa finally closed her mouth. She wiped a palm across her cheek and the tears. "Okay," she nodded and stepped away from Max's desk.

15

Rosa hurried into her car, shut the door and turned on the ignition, gasping repeatedly under the weight of her tears. It was like a knife had been sent through the walls of her chest, and it hurt deeper than any pain she could have imagined.

With tears streaming down her flushed cheeks, she got a glance towards the office window and caught Max, standing behind the curtain, peeping out at her. Angrily, she pushed the gear into reverse and stomped on the pedal. The tires shrieked backward and she whizzed out of Max's driveway.

She wept, with her hands shaking on

the wheel. She needed to get home to Bailey. The tears blinded her sight and she brushed the back of her palm across her eyes and strained her eyes to stay focused on the road.

Last night shouldn't have happened, really?

How could Max say that to her?

Didn't last night mean anything to her?

How could she make her feel so good then turn cold on her like it was nothing? Didn't she have any feelings for her?

Her heart was breaking.

This is so crazy. I have only known her a few weeks but she feels like everything to me.

Rosa made it home and Bailey was absolutely fine and delighted to see her. She collapsed onto the floor crying into Bailey's soft fur and Bailey licked at her tears.

She took Bailey out for a run. She ran as fast as she could hoping to outrun everything that was hurting her. She collapsed against a wall struggling to get her breath.

Last night had been magical? Hadn't it?

When she finally managed to get home, feed Bailey, shower and pull herself back together she knew she needed to head to the restaurant.

~

THE PARKING LOT WAS HUGE; it served as a parking lot to the different stores lined up on the block. There was a shopping complex, a spa salon, a barber saloon, a meat store, and Mr. Pablo's restaurant only served as one of the shops on the line. It was a small and surprisingly popular restaurant, selling meals at affordable prices.

Customers were walking in and out of the restaurant; while some cars pulled in, others drove away. There were pedestrians walking past, a couple holding hands and another arguing in their car, and Rosa could see them from the window of her car.

It was ten in the morning and the weather was warm with chilly fog. Rosa had only worked mornings a few times in the past, she was rarely there in the day, only coming around in the evenings to do her shifts.

Her thoughts drifted back to Max.

Max. She had touched her in a way that no one else ever had before. Rosa had never felt sex like it. Max had worshipped her body in every way.

She loved Max's raw power and strength and how dominant she was. She liked the way Max grabbed her hair and pulled her face in hard against her pussy and the way she had commanded Rosa to fuck her and to push her whole hand inside of her. Rosa had small hands but it still amazed her how her whole hand had slid inside Max and she couldn't stop thinking about how incredible it felt feeling Max orgasm on her hand, her pussy tightening and pulsing against Rosa's fist. She loved the way Max had slapped Rosa's breasts and pulled hard at her nipples—*how did she know how to be so accurate in her pressure?* Just verging on too hard, just enough to send her painful, exciting pleasures. She had noticed bruises on her body all across her breasts this morning when she got out the shower in addition to the ones around her wrists. A thrill had run through her when she saw her body marked from Max and everything Max had done to her. Her nipples brushed against her top and were sore. Good sore. Rosa shut her eyes tightly at the memories. God she wanted to do it all over again. Aside from just the sex, she wanted to be with Max. She realised she felt safe with Max and in Max's strong arms. She wanted that.

God, Rosa, shut up. Max doesn't want that.

She turned her head away from the window to look straight ahead of her. She sighted Mr. Pablo's car pulling up in his usual parking space.

Rosa banged her door shut and took hurried steps to meet Mr. Pablo.

The man had turned around and was now walking towards the entrance of the restaurant.

"Hola, Mr. Pablo."

"Rosa!" He was so shocked to see her he paused in his tracks. "What are you doing here? You didn't show up for two nights!" He held two fingers to her face. "And why are your eyes so red?" He was more disgusted than concerned.

"I slipped in my bathtub," she lied, and he ran his eyes over her body searchingly. "I hit my head, and it hurt so I-I cried."

"Do you have a doctor's note?" He flapped his palm at her.

Rosa scrunched her face. "I didn't go to the ER. I'm so sorry, sir," she quickly added, reading the disbelief in Mr. Pablo's eyes.

"This is unlike you, Rosa; you never miss your shift."

Rosa nodded quietly. At this point, she had a headache.

"Last chance!" The man shot a warning finger at her.

"Thank you, sir," Rosa said gratefully.

"And you'll work a double shift to make up for your absence."

Rosa had already expected that, she came prepared. "I will, sir."

Mr. Pablo turned around to walk away and Rosa followed on his heels.

They walked into the restaurant together, breezed past the dining area and through the double-leaf swing door that led into the kitchen. The chefs were already started at the gas stoves. The restaurant opened by 10am every morning and the kitchen was already steaming with cooking.

"Where's Noah?" yelled Mr. Pablo above the activity going on in the kitchen. "No-ah!"

"Yes, sir!" a voice unfamiliar to Rosa responded.

A man in his late thirties jogged to stand before her and Mr. Pablo, and Rosa regarded the tall, lean guy she had never seen before.

"This is Noah," Mr. Pablo said to Rosa, "He's our new chef."

Rosa nodded, acknowledging the man. He was staring at her with a plastered smile across his lips and hands held behind his back. He was dressed in the chef's white uniform.

"He started working here two days ago," continued Mr. Pablo, "and he'll be here all day, three days a week." He turned to Noah. "Noah, this is Rosa, she's one of our waitresses, she works night shifts."

Noah extended his hand to Rosa. "Nice to meet you, Rosa."

Rosa shook his hand, nodding, "Nice to meet you too. Ignore my eyes," she stated awkwardly, conscious of the glaring redness of her eyes.

Noah acknowledged her statement with a nod, still wearing his plastered smile.

"Alright," Mr. Pablo whisked around,

clapping his hands, "Everyone, get to work!"

And Noah turned around and briskly returned to his work station.

Rosa exited the kitchen. She needed to get to the locker room. She had shown up in her normal clothes, and she needed to change into the restaurant's uniform. A spare pair of shirts and aprons were kept in the locker, situated in the staff restroom so she turned around and headed in that direction.

She changed her clothes, pulled her hair into a ponytail, then proceeded to tie the apron around her waist.

Max. Her thoughts drifted to the beautiful older woman, and she shook her head to shake away the memories.

16

Max could not focus. Not a minute went by that her mind did not drift away to Rosa, she was so innocent and tender that it hurt Max to make her cry; she didn't deserve it. Someone like Rosa deserved to be cherished, loved, and protected, and Max was in the capacity to do all three, but she could not afford to become vulnerable to any woman again, not after what Caroline did. But Rosa was not like the other girls she had casual fun with, Rosa was everything a woman needed in her life; she was pure, she was young, she was gentle—heck!—she hadn't said it to her yet, but she was a brilliant writer. Her raw talent was actually blooming under Max's daily tutelage.

Only the other day she had called Kimberly- the manager at Wordflux to resend the draft that Rosa had submitted to WordFlux years ago, she had been so impressed by her input that she needed to see why they had rejected her script in the first place. And when Kimberly sent it, Max realized that it wasn't much different from the one she had received from Rosa that morning she first showed up on her front porch- it was good, raw but so much potential- but Max realized that it was originally sent barely a week after Caroline had left her. She had not been in the best frame of mind then. She didn't even remember reading it the first time. In fact, she was surprised she had ever recovered from that heartbreak. Maybe she hadn't really.

She spun in her chair.

Would Rosa be any different?

At least Caroline was within her age bracket. Rosa was so much younger and it scared her.

What would someone as young and beautiful as Rosa want with miserable old Max?

Anyway, she was supposed to be teaching Rosa, mentoring her to become a better writer, not fucking her on her desk.

Max swung the chair back around to lean forward on her desk. She entwined her fingers and held them under her chin.

She had a lot of questions, so many questions that didn't have answers, and it dawned on her, suddenly hit her, that she didn't really know Rosa—she had never really asked her many questions. Rosa had always been interested in Max, but Max had only just learnt about Rosa's dog.

Her phone rang and it snatched her out of her thoughts. She freed her hands from under her chin and looked down at the ringing phone. It was Kimberly.

"Oh shoot!" She jolted to her feet, answering the phone.

"Good afternoon, ma'am. We're ready for you," Kimberly said, and Max dropped her eyes down to her wrist.

The time was 1:40pm.

"Fine, I'll be fifteen minutes late but I'm on my way. Hold everything down for me, would you?"

"Of course, ma'am." And the phone line went dead.

Max gathered her things together into her large purse, collected her car keys, and practically ran out of her house.

God this Rosa thing is driving me crazy.

Two days and the girl had made her miss two meetings already.

Max dashed to her car and drove out into the street.

ROSA FELT EXHAUSTED. It was more of emotional and mental exhaustion than it was physical.

The morning shift was over and she was halfway into her second shift. And she would stay for the night shift- her original shift- to cover up for her absence in the past two days.

She had worked for half a day thus far so she stepped into the kitchen to get some soup. All workers were entitled to a free plate of food. If they worked for half a day, they could get something for less than $5.

And because she was working the entire day, she would be entitled to more food. A whole day of work equaled something worth $10, even though Rosa knew she might not want to consume a second plate.

Her heart was bothered and that stole her appetite, but she hadn't had anything to eat all morning, not even a cup of coffee as she had rushed out of Max's home earlier that morning. And now, her stomach was starting to churn.

"I hope you like it," Noah said as he dished some soup into her bowl. They were both standing in the kitchen by the stove. He smiled intently at her; he had been looking at her since Mr. Pablo made their acquaintance.

Stealing glances at her every time she came into the kitchen to collect a customer's order, but he wouldn't be the first man to stare longingly at her. Rosa was used to getting attention from men; she had always turned heads wherever she went, but it always made her feel so shy and awkward. She was never interested in the men, sometimes she was interested in the women, but when they realised how painfully awkward and shy she could be, it

never worked out. She had never got beyond a few dates or a quick fuck. Ever since
she started working at the restaurant, both
customers and co-workers alike would hit
on her. So she was very used to it, and like
all the other men before him, Rosa simply
ignored Noah.

"Thank you," she said and turned
around to walk out of the kitchen with the
bowl of soup fitted in her hands.

The soup was steaming hot so she blew
some air into it. She went to sit on a table
usually reserved for staff in the staff area. It
was situated just in front of the kitchen and
away from the main dining area where customers sat to eat.

Satisfied that the soup's temperature
had cooled down, she picked up her spoon
and gathered up the liquid and fed it into
her mouth. It was warm and satisfying. She
shut her eyes and felt the soothing soup as
it traveled down her throat.

"Hey." She opened her eyes to see Noah
standing over her. "Delicious?" He grinned
down at her. "I noticed you shutting your
eyes as you drank it. That good, huh?" The
thin guy grinned, exposing a set of yel-

lowish teeth that showed he had smoked one too many tobacco cigarettes.

Disturbed, Rosa picked her plate up in her arms and excused herself away from his presence.

17

"Do you like it?" Max Moore had asked her, amused by the twinkle in Caroline's eyes. She was holding Caroline's hand in her own and together, they stood in front of the Victorian home with a tag dangling down the post mount mailbox behind them that read *Sold*!

Caroline looked over at Max with her lips parted in surprise. "Is this what I think it is?" she asked, excitement lacing her voice.

Max nodded; her cheeks lifted in a broad smile.

"Oh my god!" Caroline had exclaimed,

sending her arms around her, and Max held her in an embrace and laughed.

"Wow!" Caroline jumped down from her arms.

"Let's go in, have a look!" Max dipped her hand in the back pocket of her jeans and withdrew a key.

Caroline gasped as she grabbed the key from Max. Like a little kid, she ran up the small porch stairs and Max walked behind her.

She put the key in the keyhole, turned it open, and shrugged backward excitedly at Max.

Max laughed, "Go on."

And Caroline pushed the large door open and sent her hands over her mouth. She wheeled around, her eyes taking in the large, exquisite space.

"You like it?" Max was leaning at the doorway, watching her beautiful wife.

"Yes, baby, I love it!" Caroline was excited. She ran into Max's arms, hugging her tightly. "Thank you, I love you so much!"

And Max held her in her arms, before pulling back to say, "Let's walk around, there's more." She closed the door behind them and led Caroline through the antechamber.

Together, they stepped into the front room and Caroline whizzed around, feeling the beautiful furniture. The room was well decorated with nude, subtle colors. The chairs were off-white, large, and comfortable with a matching coffee table.

Natural flowers sat in beautiful planters in different corners of the room. There was a chandelier, high on the ceiling yet long enough to dangle above the center wooden table. A fireplace sat in a corner of the walls with antique decorative pieces beautifully placed around the room.

"You got me a yellow chair?" Caroline observed happily, walking to the single sofa that sat amongst the chairs. She loved the color yellow; it was her favorite shade of all colors. And even though Max found the chair too bright, in fact, she hated it, she could not resist incorporating it into the house for the sake of Caroline.

She shrugged. "It's our home, it has to have a bit of each other, don't you think?"

"Wow!" Her eyes were still roaming the room, taking in the furniture, "It's beautiful, Max, I love it!"

"Come."

Max led the way out of the front room through the hallway. "This would be my office," she said, opening a large door that led into an airy space.

She held the door open for Caroline to step in, and once she did, she stepped in right after her.

The office had a large wooden desk, a chair, and a bookshelf sitting in the corner.

Next to the desk were a sizable printer and photocopier.

"There's not much going on in here," said Max, "I'm sure you'll help me decorate it."

Caroline smiled. "Of course, even though I think it looks good this way." She turned to look at Max. "You do most of your work at the Wordflux head office anyway."

Max walked forward to take Caroline's hands into hers, and Caroline's brows furrowed inquisitively with a suspicious grin widening the corners of her lips.

"I want to focus on us, baby," said Max.

"I've worked so hard these past years, and now that I have published *Amanda's Summer,* which has just been an absolute rollercoaster. Nobody could have predicted how well that book would be received, I want to retire from the—"

"You want to retire from writing?"

"Of course not," laughed Max, "A writer never retires. I just want to work from home, from here, so that I can have more time for you."

Caroline smiled.

"I want us to start a family, Caroline," Max said matter-of-factly. "I love you."

"I love you too," Caroline replied. "Let's see the rest of the house!" She pulled Max by the hand and Max sighed, following after her. She could only hope that this time, Caroline would be willing to carry their baby. She had been asking her for two years.

They walked out of the office and Max pointed ahead, "There's a kitchen over there, a pantry that way, and a bathroom at that end."

"It's so spacious!" commented Caroline,

"It's like double the size of our old apartment."

"Well, what can I say, things have changed significantly financially for us now. With the success of Wordflux and my novels selling like crazy. There's even talk of a movie offer for Amanda's Summer. Here there would be enough space for a child and a dog, wouldn't there?"

Caroline laughed. She took a step forward, wrapped her arms around Max's neck and kissed her deeply.

Max shuddered. Four years and she still felt chills whenever Caroline touched her.

Caroline withdrew her lips from hers to stare intently into her eyes. "I love you," she reassured Max.

And Max nodded. "I love you more."

"Now, let's go see the rest of the house."

Both women climbed up the stairs with Max continuing her descriptive tour.

CAROLINE WAS the love of Max's life. They had met at a dinner party organized by one of the famous hoteliers in town, Jake Hoffman. Max was good friends with the Hoffman family, she had actually gone to school with Jake and his brothers in the late 1980s. But she was particularly fond of Jake, hence they had kept in touch through the years.

Like her, Jake had done very well for himself and became the owner of multiple hotels across the States. On that particular night, he had hosted a dinner to celebrate the latest launching of his newest projects, which was a hotel situated on the outer part of San Francisco, and Max attended like she did most of his events. He was a dear friend and she showed up to support him and his husband, Sam, whenever she could find the time.

The dinner had been buzzing with their friends, the food was great and the music was soothing. Max was standing in a corner, chatting with one of Jake's brothers —Justin, and that was when Caroline walked up to them, and it hit her like a strike of lightning.

She watched Caroline exchange long pleasantries with Justin, an obvious friend, and Max could not help the feelings of attraction that grew so instantly inside of her.

"Hey, so Max," Justin finally said, "this is my friend Caroline, she's an interior designer here in San Francisco. She did all the designs at Jake's new hotel."

Caroline acknowledged Justin's introduction with a smile and a nod of her head.

"And this is Max Moore, an author and the owner of WordFlux publishing."

"Nice to meet you," Max extended a hand to Caroline and the smiling woman shook it.

"Max Moore," Caroline repeated thoughtfully. "*The* Max Moore that wrote *Amanda's Summer*?"

Max smiled, shrugging slightly in acknowledgment. She lifted her drink to her lips.

"I loved that book!" exclaimed Caroline. "I was glued until the end."

"Thank you." Max was pleased. The lovely Caroline had not only read but loved her work. *Could this night get any better?*

"It was a brilliant piece!"

"Thank you, I appreciate that."

"Guys, look, there goes the mayor of Los Angeles. I will be right back!" and with that, Justin was gone. He disappeared into the crowd of guests, leaving Max with Caroline.

Both women smiled warmly at each other and proceeded to take a sip from the glasses in their hands.

Caroline went on about the book and Max obliged her excited questions. By the end of the night, they had talked about books, arts, and culture. They exchanged numbers. Four days and endless texts after, Max invited her for lunch in her home, and Caroline didn't leave Max's house that night. Engrossed and unable to keep their hands off one another, they made love in Max's bed and that birthed the beginning of a romantic relationship between them. They dated in the months that followed and not a day went by that Max did not speak to her.

In six months, she had asked Caroline to move in with her, and in another six months, asked her to marry her.

It was unlike any feeling Max had ever had before. She was in love and she stopped at nothing to prove it to Caroline every day of their lives.

She gave, and gave, so much that she didn't take a second to question if she was receiving or not.

18

"Hi, Mom," Rosa spoke tiredly into her Air pods.

"How are you, baby?"

"I'm fine, Mom, just reversing out of the parking lot," she said, glancing to her sides to check for any approaching vehicles.

"You haven't called in a while."

"Yeah, I know, I've being swamped with work." She put the gear in drive and accelerated onto the road.

"Lola tells me that Max Moore woman has been giving you a hard time?"

"No, Mom, she used to, not anymore... not really anyway," her words drifted.

"Well, you know what they say, *nothing*

good comes easy so be patient and put in the work, follow her teachings, and I'm sure by the end of the day, you will have learned so much, you'll be the next famous author."

"Thanks, Mom."

"You sound really exhausted."

"I've been at work since 10am."

"Why?" Her mother was alarmed. "I thought you did night shifts."

"I do."

"So why did you have to work an entire day today?"

Memories of the past two days flashed through her mind, but she didn't dare tell her mother the true reason behind her extra hours.

"If you're having money problems—"

"No!"

"I can help."

Rosa would have to be desperate to ask her mother for money. "No, Mom, I'm fine," she insisted.

She took a swerve into the corner of a road and relaxed her back into the driver's seat, with one hand on the steering wheel and another to her forehead.

It was 10:40pm and the streets were

calm. She wondered if she would be able to do any work tonight as she was not feeling good nor particularly motivated. She had gone through the motions the entire day...

"Hello? Rosa?"

"I'm sorry, Mom, I'm just really tired." Her thoughts had drifted with her mother still hanging on the line. "How are you? Is everything okay with you and Thomas?"

"We are doing just fine, it's you I'm worried about."

"Don't worry about me, Mom. I'm fine. Simply tired from the day's work."

"Well, if you insist. I love you?"

"I love you too, Mom. Goodnight."

"Goodnight, baby."

The call went dead and Rosa made the last turn that led into her street. She drove down the narrow street and pulled up in front of her small apartment.

She would have to do some writing tonight, no matter how little. She was determined to finish rewriting that book Max had set her. She could feel herself growing as a writer with every new thing Max set her.

She climbed down from her car and

walked to the door of her apartment. Bailey was waiting on the other side of the door.

"Hey, girl," she said as she opened the door.

She squatted to the ground and allowed the dog to lick her face, wagging her tail excitedly. Lets go for a quick walk then get you some dinner.

Rosa made it back from the dog walk and headed to the kitchen followed by an excited Bailey.

"Mama was gone for the entire day, huh?" she stated, rubbing the dog. "Come on, let's get you something to eat."

She had always known that her apartment was small, but ever since she started working under Max and spending so much time at her house, the difference was always clear every time she stepped back into her studio apartment. She knew she had neglected Bailey the past 24 hours and promised herself she would be a better dog mom.

She grabbed some dog food and served it into Bailey's plastic bowl. She wasn't going to eat anything as she had already had her stomach full at the restaurant.

Her mind drifted to Noah; the chef had asked for her number as she was about to close from work. Ugh he was so creepy. And persistent. He had asked her three times and she had awkwardly made excuses. She wanted Max; she was in love with her. She knew it now more than ever. This was not lust nor some obsession of a fan. The feeling was real, it was real for her and she had never been so sure of anything in her life before, even though it had happened quickly and Max clearly did not feel the same.

Max. She hadn't stopped thinking about her all day. She wondered how she was doing, what she was doing, then immediately dismissed the concerns; Max was a strong experienced woman, she could handle herself alright. She needed to be worrying about herself and those chapters that sat unfinished on her computer.

She dropped her bag on her bed and removed her clothes and changed into her pajamas then got her MacBook out of her bag. As the system booted, she lifted a mug of hot tea to her mouth and took a sip. It burnt her tongue and she set it down immediately. Memories of Max and that woman flashed through her mind and she shook them away immediately; she was not going to do that to herself, not anymore.

Whatever life Max led before her was not her business, what mattered was the magic they had shared yesterday and as obviously as the Max was trying to push her away, Rosa did not believe what they shared meant absolutely nothing to her. Max was into it. Really into it. Max had looked at her like she was the most precious thing in the entire world. Max had held her like she would love and protect her forever. It couldn't have meant nothing and Rosa was not going to allow herself to believe that. It was special.

Something sparked between them and she knew that Max felt it too. But the older woman had been guarded from the moment she showed up on her front porch, and Rosa was convinced that there was pain or loss that had cut so deep to make her that guarded. She didn't care that she was older, the age did not matter to her at all; if anything, it turned her on.

She stretched her hand and picked up

the cup of tea, lifted it to her mouth, and gently sipped from the mug, careful not to burn her tongue a second time.

Rosa sighed as she looked at the document on her computer. She started typing.

19

The following morning, Rosa showed up on the front porch of Max's home. She let herself in as she usually did with the spare key Max had given her for work. She had brought Bailey with her because she hated leaving her for so many hours.

Rosa pushed the door open to find Magda cleaning in the front room.

"Hi, Magda," she greeted the woman as she closed the door behind her.

Magda paused to regard her, "Hello, Rosa, who is this beauty?"

"This is Bailey. I didn't want to keep

leaving her at home and I figured the big man would enjoy the company."

"Ah, I'm sure he will. He doesn't see other dogs often enough. You look so pretty in that dress."

"Thanks," Rosa answered with a smile "It was a gift from my sister, Lola," she said. Rosa loved the short dress with the floral print.

"She's got good taste," Magda stated admiringly.

"Oh! She's quite the fashionista."

"Obviously!"

Just then, Diablo wandered in and barked at Bailey. His tail stiffened as Bailey ran over to him then rolled on her back. Diablo sniffed her all over and then wagged his tail. Rosa called them both to the back door and let them out in the yard together. Bailey started running round like crazy and Diablo looked delighted as he tried to chase her.

"Oh its so nice to see Diablo look so happy with a friend. It was a great thing you did, restocking his food the other day," acknowledged Magda. "Ms. Max had no idea. She was very pleased and I never got to thank you."

Rosa smiled. "It was nothing really."

And Magda smirked. She returned her focus to the fireplace and resumed her cleaning.

The dogs continued playing outside, Bailey teasing Diablo constantly. He had a new lease of life suddenly.

Rosa opened the door to the office and it was empty; Max was not there yet. She glanced down at her wristwatch and the time read 9:00 am, Max was usually here by this time.

"Max," Rosa called to Magda, with a finger pointing backward, "She's not in yet?"

"Oh! She dashed out a few minutes before you got here. She'll be back."

"Rosa is here," Magda informed Max as she stepped through the door. "She is in the backyard with playing with the dogs."

"Dogs plural?" Max asked.

"She brought her dog Bailey with her.

Diablo is loving the company. They are getting along like a house on fire."

" Oh, okay. Here," She handed her a bag of groceries, "Sort these in the kitchen, will you?"

"Sure." Magda received the bag and turned towards the kitchen.

As she walked away, Max unwrapped her scarf from around her neck and hung it on the wall-mounted coat hook in the hallway. Then, she walked into her office. She noticed Rosa's stuff and her heart skipped a bit, she felt nervously excited. Ignoring her emotions, she walked to her desk and sat down in the big chair.

She flipped her computer open and went straight to her inbox. She scrolled through her emails and begun to respond to each of them. As she worked, her eyes kept darting towards Rosa's desk; she was eager to see her yet determined to hide her emotions when she did finally show up. Her ears were alert, waiting on when she would hear Rosa's voice, her footsteps, or the sound of the dogs.

She missed Rosa, she had missed her all through yesterday, and at night, when she returned home from her meeting, she sat by her fireplace, staring into the fire as she sipped on a glass of wine. She weighed the situation with Rosa in her heart. She pondered on her feelings and finally replayed the episode with Caroline on that cold November night and she decided, made up her mind, that her stance with Rosa was final.

She could not bear to allow her heart to be broken again. Besides, Rosa was much too young, a woman her age was indecisive and still had a lot of choices to make. Choosing to be with an older woman may not be one of those choices, Max was almost sure of it.

Max heard the back door opening and Rosa talking happily to the dogs.

She was here!

She adjusted herself in her chair then watched as the door to the office pushed open.

Rosa's feet paused on seeing her, almost as if she was not expecting her to be back. She hesitated, before continuing into the room.

"Good morning, I um, I brought my dog

with me. I hope that's ok. Only I didn't want to leave her at home on her own anymore and Diablo loves her. I left them in the yard for a bit, its a nice day."

"Thats fine, Rosa. You should have brought her with you from the start. Of course I wouldn't want her to be at home alone."

"I wasn't sure," Rosa muttered and tucked her hair behind her ears.

Max watched as Rosa looked down to the floor and walked awkwardly to her desk. When she sat down, Max asked her, "Do you want to work on the other chapters today?"

"I did two last night," Rosa responded. "I will email them right away." She avoided her eyes as she spoke.

"That was fast," Max noted.

"I worked overnight after I finished at the restaurant."

Max sighed, "How did it go with your manager?"

Rosa was still not looking at her. Her hands were now busy on the computer. "It was okay, I did extra shifts in the day to make up for the lost time."

Max nodded.

"I've sent them to you."

"Yeah." She shifted her eyes from Rosa down to her computer.

Sensing her distraction, Rosa finally rolled her eyes up from her desk to look at her, properly. She had only stolen a glance when she walked in earlier, now she could watch her, looking at her computer. She had on a light blue suit with a black button down shirt and her hair slicked back. Her reading glasses were sitting across her face and her lips looked so full and inviting.

Her lips...

Rosa remembered how they had kissed her, *everywhere,* and she tingled in excitement at the memories. Max was so close, so close yet so far away.

She bit her lower lip and dropped her gaze. She had work to do, more chapters to complete, so she opened the file and resumed her editing and rewriting.

She would leave on time, later on, to go and work her shift at the restaurant. The restaurant was her major source of income, her only source actually, and she could not afford to lose that job. She wouldn't want to have to fall back on her mom or her rich sister. She didn't like to bother her family with her finances; when money became too tight, she simply found other jobs to complement what she was paid at the restaurant, or she worked extra shifts. But she was not much of a spender anyway, so she rarely ran into debt.

She didn't run after the fancier and more expensive things of life other women her age might. She was content with just the basic things of life and so far, she was doing okay. One day maybe, if she got to get published and successfully sell a book, she'll make enough money to go on a trip. She had always wanted to visit Anne Frank's house in Amsterdam.

For now, she had chapters to complete and submit to her teacher, Max.

"This is great, really great, Rosa!" Max said, peeling her glasses away from her face.

She leaned back into her chair and regarded Rosa with a smile. "You're really getting so good. I'm so proud of you."

Rosa smiled up briefly at her from her keypad. "Thank you."

"You should be proud of yourself."

"I am," she said genuinely. She smiled up at Max one more time before lowering her gaze down again.

Max pointed her glasses in Rosa's direction and said, "I can't wait to see what you'll do with the remaining chapters." She sat back up in her chair and put her glasses back on her face. "Good girl."

And Rosa smiled, she yearned to hear those words from Max. She felt the twinge from them run right through her body and stop between her legs.

I'd be the best girl you could ever imagine, Max.

20

The following few weeks went by routinely.

Rosa showed up to work every morning with Bailey, took Diablo and Bailey for a walk or played with them in the yard, made Max coffee when she agreed for her to do so, came back to the office to work on different drafts and scripts as assigned by Max. At the close of work, by 2 pm, she would call it a day and return to the restaurant to do her night shifts. Noah still followed her around, wooing her relentlessly. He kept an extra bowl of soup and tried to give her preferential treatment every time he was on duty.

She had given him her phone number because he would't stop asking and he made it a duty to send her memes and relentless texts almost every day despite her barely replying.

Max had not talked about them nor the moment they shared that night. It was like things had gone back to normal, to the way they used to be between them; purely work, only this time around, Max was much softer and kinder to her.

She didn't yell or speak harshly to her, she conversed normally, correcting her mistakes and teaching her the ropes of writing, and Rosa had to admit, she was learning a great deal from the woman. Max also started talking to her about her life, her family, her previous relationships, everything really and Rosa enjoyed opening up to her. They would sit and take lunch together for an hour every day and they would talk. Max even started talking about herself. She changed the subject when it came to her previous relationships which reinforced Rosa's theory about Max's pain. But otherwise, Max was open with her and it was beautiful. Everything was fine, except that she couldn't stop thinking about what had happened between them, and she always wondered if Max thought about their moment too. There were nights that Rosa would dream the sex, and countless moments that she would touch herself to the thoughts of Max and she came, she always came hard and then felt gutted right afterward.

The waiting was eating her up, but she dared not make an advance like she did the first time. Max had been very direct, that it could not happen a second time, she had been as clear as day and as much as sometimes—most times—Rosa just wanted to reach out and touch her, just touch her strong hand, but she could not gather the courage to do so. Weeks had gone by, weeks of working and talking.

Tonight, as Rosa lay in her bed, reminiscing about what had happened and how things had now become, she sighed and turned on her side. It was about two in the morning, and she had climbed into her bed only about thirty minutes earlier.

She tossed again, images of Max racing through her head.

Frustrated with the longing, she slipped her hand under her duvet and into the trousers of her pajamas.

She was wet. Warm too.

Unable to resist the urge, she let her fingers linger and shut her eyes.

Her fingers moved in circles around her clitoris, warm and aroused, she spread her thighs further apart and continued to move her fingers in circular motions.

She imagined Max's tongue in the place of her fingers, licking her in upward strokes, and Max's fingers deep inside of her.

And she slipped two fingers downward and into the entrance of her vagina, just like she imagined Max would do.

She slipped them back out to settle on her clitoris, the apex of all pleasures, and her back arched under her fingers. Her eyes were shut tight with memories and images of Max, and she cried pleasurably at the electrifying delight that swam through her body.

Her hips rocked faster against her fingers. She pressed her left hand over her right hand to increase the pressure on her clitoris. Her toes curled downward and she squeezed her thighs tightly against her fingers. This always took her over the edge in no time. She could feel her walls tightening, the orgasm was building and she increased the speed of her fingers against her clit until she could feel her body erupt into rapture and she yelped as she exploded into an orgasm.

Loudly, she breathed out through her mouth and her hips collapsed down into the bed. She pulled a pillow into her embrace and sent a thigh over the soft foam. Cuddling it closely, she shut her eyes and drifted off into sleep.

ON THE OTHER side of town, barely an hour away, Max was watching a private strip show inside an exclusive LGBT clubhouse. It was an all-white party, organized for the crème de la crème members of the society, and Max, breezy on vodka, had two of the strippers giving her a private dance in one of the side rooms. The music was blasting in the main hall, easily heard in their private room, and Max sat on the love seat. A blonde and a brunette stripped to their thongs in front of her. They were gyrating with their pussys so close to Max's face, she could smell them.

Max toyed with the idea of asking the women home with her. They were beautiful, they were young, she could lose herself in mindlessly fucking them.

But a flash of Rosa's beautiful face appeared on her mind, smiling and moaning under her. It was Rosa she wanted so badly. Only Rosa.

ROSA'S GATHERED her stuff into her backpack. It was a Friday afternoon and she was ready to go home. She had impressed Max so much with her work that the other day the older woman had cut her closing time to 1:30pm instead of 2pm.

In her words, "You need some time to yourself; you work really hard. Take the extra minutes to visit a friend, get a pedicure, or just relax with Bailey."

"You love her so much don't you?"

"I do," Rosa had smiled proudly, "She's my baby."

"Same as Diablo is mine. Big baby, but baby nonetheless!" Max had said, smiling sadly. "Do you want children, Rosa?"

Rosa was surprised by the question, but answered straight away. "Oh for sure. Absolutely. I would love to be a mom. I want to look after my babies, play with them, teach them, give them the world." Rosa smiled. She really did want children one day. "Did you ever think about having children?" she fired back to Max not really expecting an answer.

"I did. So badly at one time. But it wasn't to be. I wish things had been different." Max looked contemplative.

"It's still possible you know? Anything is possible."

"Unlikely, Rosa, but possible, yes. I would need to be with the right person I think. I work too much to do it alone."

That was two days ago.

Now, Rosa, with her laptop, the charger, her cellphone, and notes gathered into her bag at exactly 1:30pm, swung the bag over her shoulder and proceeded to walk out of the office to find Bailey.

She could hear Max's voice coming from the end of the hallway talking to the dogs. Rosa followed her voice and it led her into the kitchen. Her eyes popped in surprise when she saw Max standing in an apron, slicing vegetables on a chopping board.

Rosa laughed.

"What?" Max taunted her, "You've never seen a grown woman cooking before?"

Rosa was amused. "I have, but not you."

"Yeah," Max smiled back at her. "It's my mom's birthday today—"

"Aww!"

"We always cooked lunch together on each of her birthdays," Max said, gesticulating the knife in her hand in the air before returning her hand down to the chopping board. "Even when she was in the ER during her last days, I still made lunch and took it to her." She shrugged, smiling sadly. "She couldn't eat it, but she was just glad I was there, with the food."

Rosa's heart melted. "What did you make?"

"Tacos!" she said, and Rosa chuckled. "Chicken taquitos, fried crispy, served on a bed of lettuce topped with sauce, salsa, and cheese. It was her favorite dish."

"Was she Mexican?"

Max shook her head. "She loved a Mexican man, but they never got married."

Rosa watched Max in admiration, unable to relax the sad smile that sat across her lips. She had come to say goodbye, but now she stood glued to the doorway.

"So, seven years later and I still make this same dish, every birthday, and eat it like she was still here." She paused and stared sadly ahead into the bare space. "I miss her, every day. She was all I had, until my ex wife, Caroline. Losing each of them broke my heart." She turned her head sideways and Rosa could see that she was holding back the tears that welled up in her eyes. She resumed cutting her veggies.

Rosa stepped further into the kitchen, she walked to stand next to her. Gently, she reached her hand over Max's and brought it down on top of hers.

Max turned slowly to stare at her.

With their eyes locked, Rosa swallowed hard then asked, "May I help?"

Max held her gaze. Seconds felt like minutes with Rosa's hand still placed on top of hers. She could see the lingering pain in her eyes, and she knew she would cherish this vulnerable moment of hers, forever.

Finally, the Max nodded, sliding her hand away from underneath hers. She stepped back and Rosa stood in her position then she turned away and walked to the sink. "I'll go heat the skillet."

And together, they cooked. They chatted lightly. Rosa cherished that moment because she suddenly felt so much closer to Max. Just the mere act of doing something as simple as cooking, occasionally bumping into each other, with their fingers brushing, stolen gazes, and swift smiles with the dogs scuttling round their feet, made her want to stay, and remain this way with her, forever.

Twenty-five minutes went by and both women stood back to look gladly at the meal they had prepared. They exchanged pleased glances and Max moved to the cabinet and begun to pull out tablemats and cutlery.

"Here," Rosa breezed to her side, "I'll take those." Their fingers brushed as she received the items from Max. Ignoring the tingling sensation it brought her, she asked, "Where should I set these?"

The house had a dining area both in the kitchen and in an adjourned area of the living room.

"The living room, please."

"Okay." And Rosa walked away, out of the kitchen, down the hallway, and into the dining area, adjourned to the living room.

She set the placemats down, arranged the cutlery then made a trip back into the kitchen for the food.

"I'll grab the plates and wine," Max said as Rosa lifted the bowl of food in her hands.

She walked out of the kitchen with Max following closely behind. When they reached the dining table, Max arranged two plates with two glasses of wine and Rosa wondered who she was expecting.

She glanced down at her wristwatch and the time read 2pm.

Max caught her reading her time. "Is it 4pm yet?" she asked her.

"No, I still have two hours left."

Max nodded. "Rosa?" she called just as the girl turned around to head back into the kitchen.

"Yes," she answered, pausing in her steps to turn back around and face Max.

"Thank you for helping me set this up."

"Sure, no problem. I'll just go grab the water and then be on my way."

Max sighed. "Would you please stay?"

"Me?" She put a finger to her chest and Max could not help the chuckle that escaped her lips.

"Of course, you."

Rosa was surprised.

"I usually have this lunch alone, it used to be just me and her, and then it became just me, but I don't want to be alone today. Please stay? But I mean, if you have to be at the restaurant earlier than usual or you have other things to do, I'll understand—"

"Are you kidding me? It will be an honor to have this lunch with you."

"Really?"

"Oh my god, yes! Thank you for inviting me."

"Okay."

Max chuckled, and Rosa chuckled too. Both women exchanged glances and laughed.

"Go get the water then."

"Sure," Rosa agreed and whisked to the kitchen to fetch two bottles of water and glasses.

Max was waiting on her feet, putting finishing touches to their setup.

"Ready?" she asked as Rosa emerged from the kitchen with hands full.

"Definitely," she said, placing the water on each of their sides, followed by the glasses.

"Let's sit then." Max lowered herself down unto the chair and Rosa followed suit.

21

The women sat down to a quiet dinner. Rosa could tell that Max had a lot on her mind; her gaze was blank, picking only lightly at her food. Sometimes her fork twirled in the food for minutes before she lifted a slice of taco to her mouth.

Rosa had never seen her this way before.

She ate her food, doing her best to match Max's pace. Sometimes, all a person needed was a soul who would sit with them and understand the silence.

"I'm sorry," Max apologized, looking up at Rosa. "It's usually a tough day for me."

"It's okay," Rosa murmured. "Do you have any siblings?" she added after a few minutes.

"I wish I did," Max chuckled sadly. "I was her only child."

Rosa nodded quietly, careful not to ask so much even though her heart was burning with a lot of questions.

"Tell me about your sister," Max said.

Rosa nodded. "I have a sister, Lola. She lives in Miami."

"What does she do?"

"She's a news anchor, she's quite successful."

"And you're the author."

Rosa chuckled shyly, pushing strands of hair behind her ears with her gaze down on her plate. "Not yet but, hopefully, someday."

"You will," Max's nod was assuring and Rosa sprung her head up in awe. "We'll get your manuscript published. Its good, you know. I'm sorry I didn't tell you earlier. There are a few things we can improve, but the story is good."

She could not believe her ears. "Wo-wow!" she stammered, tears tickling the corners of her eyes, "I-I don't know what to say."

Max smiled and returned her gaze down to her plate.

"Thank you, thank you so much!"

"You did it, it's all you. You should be proud."

"You brushed me up," insisted Rosa.

"Well, you know what they say, iron sharpens iron." She lifted her gaze to smile at Rosa, just as one tear escaped down the young woman's cheek.

"Thank you." Rosa's lips trembled. "Can I go call my mom? I'm sorry but I need to tell her."

"Sure, go ahead."

"Thank you." She pushed her chair backward and jumped up on her feet.

Max watched her as she hastened down the hallway and disappeared into the kitchen.

Minutes later, she could overhear Rosa faintly talking excitedly over the phone, and Max smiled to herself. Rosa was the second writer she would be giving an opportunity to that year.

When Rosa reemerged, Max was on her

feet, gathering the plates from the table.

"Thank you so much," Rosa said, clasping her hands together.

"You're most welcome," Max spoke with her eyes focused on the chore before her.

"I'll go grab some bowls for the left-over." With that, Rosa turned back around and walked back to the kitchen.

"It's past 3:00," Max observed, "You should head off to get ready for work now. I don't want to make you late."

Rosa instinctively dropped her eyes down to her wrist, confirming the time. She had enjoyed being with Max so much that she had lost track of time.

"What will you do for the rest of the day?" she asked Max.

"Read manuscripts."

"Right!" Rosa laughed.

"I'll be fine," she said seriously. "Don't worry about me."

Rosa nodded. She hesitated on her feet, conflicted on whether to turn around and face the door or take three strides forward and hug Max, who was staring at her as if waiting for her to decide.

Damning all reason, she charged for-

ward and put her arms around an unsus-
pecting Max, and Rosa didn't even care that
she didn't hug her back.

"Goodnight," Rosa spoke into her chest
before taking a step backward to tuck her
hair behind her ears.

Max nodded and half-smiled.

Rosa turned around and dashed towards the kitchen where she had left her
bag. She collected the backpack and
walked back out to find Rosa standing at
her bar and pouring herself a drink.

Without saying another word, knowing
that she had already said her goodbyes,
Rosa called Bailey and walked down the
entrance of the house and when she got to
the front door, she turned the knob and exited the building.

Max watched her leave. She heard the
sound of the door shutting behind Rosa
and Bailey and saw Diablo as he strolled
into the front room. Max walked around
her mini-bar with her drink in hand. She
went to her TV cabinet, pulled one of the
drawers open, and retrieved an old photo
album. With both her hands full, she sat on

one of the sofas. Diablo immediately jumped on the sofa with her.

She reached her hand across the arm of the sofa and carefully placed her glass of wine on the side stool beside it. Then, she pulled the throw blanket over her feet, up to her waist, and flipped the photo album open.

A sad smile ran across her lips as she stared at a photo of her mother, holding her as a baby in a small hospital bed. She was naked, newly born with vernix caseosa still evidently coated all over her skin, and her mother, with her vibrant red hair and hospital gown, was holding her to her chest, staring into her face and crying joyfully.

22

"Hi, Erin!" Rosa greeted as she breezed into the staff area of the restaurant.

"Hi, Rosa!" Erin's face was glued to her cellphone. "Check this out!"

Erin showed her a Tiktok video and Rosa laughed

"You better not let Mr. Pablo catch you on your phone," Noah warned Erin.

"Well, he's not here yet," defended Erin, "besides, there are barely any customers right now"

"They'll come," he said then added, "Hi, Rosa."

"Whatever!" Erin rolled her eyes and

dropped her phone into the pocket of her apron.

"Hi, Noah, how are you?" Rosa smiled at him.

"I'm great," Noah replied, excited at her friendly demeanor towards him.

"Let's go see if there are any tables we need to clear," Rosa suggested, and both women started to walk out of the staff area.

"You're in pretty high spirits today, you even started conversation with creepy Noah." Erin observed.

"Yeah," Rosa beamed, "It's been a wonderful day!"

Erin nodded with a smile, knowing that there was no use asking further questions because Rosa would only share the details if she felt like it.

Both women walked around the tables and busied themselves. Minutes clocked into hours and Rosa waltzed through her job. She was over the moon!

Not only did Max agree to publish her book, but Max had shared things with her; she felt so much closer to her. She could only hope that this new emotional closeness had come to stay.

B‍Y THE END of the night, with spirits still
high and a plastered smile across her face,
Rosa waved goodnight to Erin as the girl
begged to leave a few minutes earlier to
make it in time for a family get-together.
Mr. Pablo had left much earlier and so did
some of the staff. Rosa walked into the
dining area and flipped the sign to *Close*.
She drew the curtain over the windows.

"Goodnight, Rosa!"

"Goodnight, Justin!"

"Bye, Rosa!"

"Bye, Maria!

"Have a great one, Rosa!"

"See you tomorrow, Mr. Hawkins." She
bade the staff goodbye as each of them
hailed her on their way out.

Finished from the dining area, she
switched off the lights then walked into the
kitchen. Satisfied that all was as it should
be, she turned off the lights and walked out
of the kitchen and towards the staff area to
collect her purse and her car keys.

As she stepped into the staff area and
pulled her locker open, Noah emerged

from one of the toilets. He set his gaze on her and began to trudge towards her.

"Oh, hi Noah!" Rosa said, observing his presence. "I didn't know you were still here." She pulled her bag from her locker and begun to search inside for her car keys.

Her bag was usually full with a laptop, flash drives, chargers, and makeup. It was always easy for her keys, which she still hadn't bought a significant keyholder for, to get missing somewhere among the pile of things.

"Yes!" she rejoiced as her fingers felt the keys. She snatched them out and turned around to leave and her mouth yelped in fear at the sight that met her eyes, and her bag went crashing to the ground. Noah was pushing his pants down while staring at her and taking closer steps towards her.

Rosa's eyes widened, she froze against the locker in fear. "What are you doing?"

"You know you want this. We are alone now. You are all mine." His trousers dropped to the floor and he moved in just his boxers. He dipped his hand into his briefs and Rosa looked away in disgust.

"Don't do this, Noah." She was crippled in fear; she couldn't move.

"I see how you've been smiling at me all day at the restaurant. I see those little dresses you wear."

Rosa's eyes burned. Her neck was completely craned to the side, refusing to look at an approaching Noah.

She snapped and snatched her bag from the floor. She made a dash for the door and Noah gripped her by the hand. She whisked backward and reacted by biting into his arm and slamming her bag across his face.

Noah winced in pain while Rosa escaped out of the staff area. Her heart thundered in her chest as she ran through the dining area with Noah running after her. "Come back here, you bitch!"

Rosa sighted a jug of water forgotten on one of the tables, so she knocked it to the floor and heard as Noah slipped over it and fell on his butt. "Fucking bitch! I'll get you!"

She pulled the entrance door open and ran out into the parking lot. She hastened towards her car, double-clicking the remote as she ran. When her hands grabbed the car handle, she pulled it open and jumped inside the vehicle. She was scared and confused.

She succeeded in starting the car and roughly drove out into the road. She was upset and almost blinded with tears. She found herself driving towards Max's house and when she pulled up in her driveway, she scrambled into her bag and grabbed her cellphone, headlights blaring brightly.

She dialed Max, looking over her shoulders, too afraid to step out of the car lest Noah had followed her.

"He attacked me, Noah, he tried to assault me. I'm scared. I'm really scared I don't know what to do." she wept into the phone.

"What? Where are you?"

"I'm here!" and she honked her car.

Max walked to her window and when she looked down and saw Rosa, she yelled into the phone, "Hang on, I'll be right there!" With that, she ended the call and dashed into her closet.

∾

MAX WAS FURIOUS. How dare this Noah try
and attack Rosa. Sweet, lovely, kind Rosa.
She snatched a pair of jeans and pulled
them up her waist followed by a tee-shirt
and boots. She ran down the stairs with Diablo barking alertly at the bottom of the
stairs.

"Stay there!" she ordered the dog and
ran out into her driveway.

She knocked on Rosa's car window
and Rosa unlocked the car, crying
profusely.

"Scoot over!" Max ordered her and Rosa
obeyed.

Max jumped into the driver's seat, the
muscles on her arms tensing up. "Where is
that restaurant?" she demanded, reversing
out into the road.

"Outside my neighborhood. Take the
turn down the road."

The tires screeched rudely against the
pavement as Max followed Rosa's direc-
tions, and in twenty-five minutes they were
pulling up in front of the restaurant.

Max was breathing through her nose,
her body vibrating in a load of rage. She
sighted a lean man locking up the main en-

trance of the restaurant and she turned to Rosa, "Is that him?"

Rosa nodded, slipping down into the car seat. Her body was quivering and Max could not contain her anger. She made to jump from the car and Rosa stopped her. "Don't leave me," she pleaded, and the pain in her eyes stirred Max even more.

"I will never let anyone hurt you." With that, she jumped out of the car, and Rosa's head peeked up curiously.

Max was running towards Noah. She reached him just as he turned around. Before he could understand what was going on, Max sent a blow under his chin and the man staggered backward.

She grabbed hold of him and threw him up against the wall, her hand on his throat, her rage white hot.

"Don't you EVER touch Rosa or any other woman again. Don't you ever expose yourself to a woman ever again. You are a spineless fucking idiot and a fucking waste of air. If I ever hear anything like this about you again, I will find you and I will rip your fucking balls clean off your body. Do you understand?"

The man's eyes were wide with fear and he could only nod cowardly in anguish.

"And Rosa- she is never coming back here!"

She dropped him to the ground and spat on him. Then she marched back to the car.

As soon as she climbed into the vehicle, Rosa wrapped her arms around her neck and Max hugged her back tightly.

"Let's go home," Max said after multiple minutes. "You'll never work in this shit hole anymore. I'll look after you now."

With that, she edged Rosa back into her seat and pulled the seatbelt across her body. She started the car and drove back to her house in Pacific heights.

She lifted Rosa into her arms and carried her into the house. She climbed up the stairs and laid Rosa quietly in her bed. She removed her shoes and gently removed the rest of her clothing, observing her body for any scratch and injuries. "Did he touch you?" she asked her tenderly.

Rosa shook her head, still upset and shuddering in fear.

"Shh, it's okay, baby. You are safe with me."

She removed her jeans and climbed into the bed beside Rosa.

She dragged the sheets over them and pulled Rosa into her embrace. She wrapped her arms around her and rubbed her hair and Rosa shuddered sobs on her chest until she drifted off to sleep.

MAX DROVE to Rosa's apartment the next morning and collected Bailey to come and stay at Max's. She nursed Rosa for the next two days, tending to her every need herself. She didn't allow Rosa to lift a finger to do anything, even her bathing was done tenderly by Max. Max knelt next to her while she was in the bath and washed her all over with a sponge. It was the most intimate act. Max shampooed her hair and massaged her scalp. And although Rosa was in no way physically hurt, Max was determined to nurture her wounded emotions until she was strong enough to face the world again. So, she kept her, lovingly grooming her back to health and being there to hold her every night and protect her.

ROSA FELT SO safe and loved in Max's presence and as she felt better, she was determined to get back to work on her writing.

What's happening with you, Max? What is this between us?

"Are you sure?" Max asked her, staring intently into her eyes as they lounged on her sofa by the fireplace, sipping coffee.

Rosa's feet were stretched out across Max's thighs, and the older woman placed a magazine on them with her coffee clasped in her right hand.

"Because you don't have to rush anything," she assured Rosa.

Rosa smiled understandingly. "My mind is in a better place now, I can write."

Max had done everything to take care of her, but not take advantage of her, and her restraint made Rosa long for her even more. She didn't know if Max was still holding on to her old rule or she was simply giving her time to heal; she hoped it was the latter. They had gotten so close this past week and now there they were, with her toes kneaded by Max's firm yet tender fingers.

This couldn't be just platonic care. *It couldn't be!*

"Fine," Max said, "You'll begin tomorrow then."

"Tonight," Rosa insisted.

"Tomorrow."

"Tonight, I need something to do." She scrunched her face and pouted her lips like a baby.

Max chuckled, "Fine."

And Rosa wiggled her feet in Max's hands.

Both women stared at each other and giggled.

THAT NIGHT, Rosa excused herself and went down into the home office with Max insisting to see her off. The woman was doting on her even though Rosa genuinely felt better.

"Oh no," Max declined as Rosa walked

towards her desk. "Please, use mine. It's much more comfortable."

Rosa smiled sweetly and switched lanes. She walked to the large, soft chair and sat into it; she twirled around comfortably then paused to smile up at Max. "True, it is much more comfortable."

Max nodded. "I'll check on you." With that, she walked away, leaving the door open.

Rosa, still smiling sheepishly, flipped her laptop open and sent her fingers on the keypad.

She could do this in one night. She had a sex scene to write- it wouldn't be that long. She could finish in a couple of hours and be back cosy in bed with Max.

So, she went to work, inspired by the woman who had come to be the love of her life.

23

The next day, Rosa slept late in the morning, having stayed up late to write. It felt good, fulfilling even, to be able to write again—and exciting, because she had completed the sex scene that was a challenge as a writer. She wanted to capture the emotions around the sex. She wanted the sex to be so much more than just sex.

She got dressed and busied herself around the house. She took a walk with Bailey and Diablo, the two dogs had become the best of friends and seemed glad to have the companionship of each other.

Rosa felt comfortable, happy being

tended to by Max, but she had no idea how much longer this was going to last. As far as Max was concerned, Rosa should not be by herself, she needed time to "heal" even though Rosa was convinced that she was fine, now. It was shocking and scary what had happened with Noah, but he hadn't actually touched her. She could go back home and do very well, but she knew she didn't want to. She was so happy living with Max.

By evening, Rosa and Max fed the dogs then retired upstairs to Max's bedroom.

"Is the sex scene in there? Max asked as Rosa moved her laptop onto her thighs.

"Yes, I finished yesterday."

Max was impressed. "Read it out to me."

Rosa flushed. "You've never asked me to read a scene out loud to you before."

Max smiled. "I'm asking now."

Rosa smiled nervously. Yet, a part of her was excited because she knew what the content of the story held. She flipped the laptop open and opened the file.

"Hold on, let me fetch a glass of wine for this. You want one?"

Rosa nodded and Max disappeared downstairs. She resurfaced, holding two glasses of wine in her hands. She handed one to Rosa, then climbed into the bed and laid on her side.

Rosa watched her drink from her cup as she drank from hers too.

"Go on!" Max nudged her.

Rosa placed the glass on the bedside stool, cleared her throat then begun to read. She told the story of a fantasy held by an assistant, about an older butch dominant woman who was her boss. It described in erotic words, how the assistant, butt naked, went around serving the older woman in every way she desired. Eventually, the assistant dropped naked on her knees and curled up at her boss's feet. She rubbed the older woman's feet and kissed up the leg of her jeans. Doing everything the older woman demanded.

Max's eyes grew dark with desire as she watched Rosa read those words.

Finished, Rosa clapped her laptop close and smiled, shrugging her shoulders. She felt almost embarrassed because she knew that Max could tell the story was a real fantasy.

Now Max was staring intently at her with one elbow to the bed, supporting her head and the other hand, clasping her wine. Rosa wished she would just say something, anything at all! Her silence was tripling her anxiety.

Finally, Max muttered, "Is that what you want?"

Rosa's cheeks flushed, she bit at her lower lip, tucked strands of dangling hair behind her ears, and nodded fervently.

"I think about it sometimes," Rosa said.

"Well, tomorrow is Magda's day off. Tomorrow, you will show up for work naked and serve my every desire. Do you understand?"

"Yes, Ma'am."

"Good girl."

Rosa's face flushed bright red.

Max knelt up in the bed. She reached forward and placed her drink next to Rosa's glass. Then, she peeled the MacBook away from Rosa's lap and kissed her hard on the mouth.

Finally!

And Rosa melted into her.

Their mouths met with the passion of the build up from the past few weeks. Max placed her hands on the sides of her head and kissed her even more passionately. She licked her nose, kissed her eyes, and ran her tongue over her ears.

Rosa moaned as shivers ran right through her body. Max's mouth felt incredible. Max lowered her lips and kissed the sides of Rosa's neck. Rosa hissed pleasurably. Leaning back, Max removed Rosa's nightdress from her body, leaving her naked. Her eyes roamed over Rosa's chest, taking in her essence; her taut nipples and supple skin. She stroked light fingers across Rosa's chest and the younger woman shivered excitedly. Max grabbed her neck and kissed her hard on the mouth.

She climbed down from the bed and pulled Rosa down the bed too. Together, they stood on the floor of her bedroom with Rosa stark naked and Max still dressed in her trouser pajamas.

"Grab me that chair," she ordered Rosa.

Rosa moved around the large bed and

dragged the ladder-back chair from the table in the corner.

"I said grab not drag."

"Yes, ma'am," Rosa responded, lifting the chair up the floor.

She brought it to where Max stood and placed it on the floor, beside her. She took a bow and took a few steps backward.

Max sat down with her legs apart. "Pass me that wine."

Rosa hastened to the bed stool and collected her glass of wine, then hurried back to hand it to her. This was turning her on!

"Feed me."

"Yes. ma'am." Rosa held the wine to Max's mouth and she drank it.

She stood back with the wine in hand and Max stared at her, wearing a serious face "Put the wine on the table and get on your knees at my feet."

Rosa obeyed hastily, feeling the warm moisture as it built up between her thighs.

She sat down on the floor of Max's feet and began to rub her leg through her cotton pajama pants. She slid the pants up to her knee and kissed her skin, gasping hungrily.

Max reached her hands down and touched Rosa's breast. She pulled her nipple hard and Rosa's body responded and she moaned loudly. Max pulled Rosa to her feet and brought her to sit on her lap in a straddling position.

"We will play your kinky boss fantasy tomorrow properly at work. But, for now, I just want to enjoy your body."

Max rose from the chair with Rosa in her arms, walked to the large sofa by the window, and placed her on it. Then she stood in front of her.

"Undress me," she ordered.

Rosa peeled her pants off first then removed her shirt, stretching up to pull it over her head. Finally, they were both naked.

"Wait here," Max demanded then walked into her bathroom. And Rosa waited, dizzy with desire. When Max reemerged from the bathroom, she had a black leather harness strapped to her hips with a dildo protruding forth.

Rosa's eyes twinkled excitedly.

"You like this?"

"I've never done it before.. but I love it. I

want to feel you fuck me with it." Rosa gasped excitedly.

Max walked over to the sofa and pushed Rosa forward over the arm of the chair.

She climbed onto the sofa and leaned forward, her bare breasts hot on Rosa's back. She licked her neck, up to her ears, nibbling her earlobes. As she sent waves of pleasure through Rosa with her kisses, her fingers slid down over Rosa's hips and in between her warm thighs. "Oh, you're so wet, baby."

Excited by her arousal, Max guided the head of the dildo to Rosa's wetness and pushed it inside her. Rosa gasped.

The dildo was thick, but slick with Rosa's wetness, slid effortlessly into her.

"That feels so good!" she cried. She felt like Max was taking her, owning her, claiming her body by fucking her this way.

Max lifted her chest from Rosa's back to kneel properly behind Rosa. She placed both hands on Rosa's hips and observed in admiration as Rosa's full dark hair was sprawled sideways on the sofa and Max thought she was the most beautiful woman she had ever seen.

She inched her hips backward and thrust back inside her. Rosa moaned into the arm of the L-shaped sofa. She rammed her hips in and out of Rosa, enjoying watching her cry softly in enjoyment. She pulled Rosa down on the sofa so that she was lying flat on her stomach. With the dildo still inside her, Max trailed her fingers around Rosa's hips and she inched backward, giving Max's fingers some space to slid down and touch her clitoris.

Rosa gasped; this was a dual pleasure.

Max's body was heavy on her back with the dildo filling her pussy. Her hips moved in and out of her in swift, experienced thrusts as her fingers rolled slick with wetness against Rosa's clitoris.

"Oh, yes!" Rosa cried, "Oh, Max!"

Her body was gyrating, lost in speechless pleasure.

"I'm going to come," Rosa suddenly announced. She felt the waves of pleasures course through her and she erupted, catapulting into orgasm. Rosa cried loudly collapsing into the sofa. With eyes pressed shut and lips wide apart, her body stiffened under Max.

Max pulled her hand from underneath her and gently slipped out of her. Rosa was limp on the couch, completely flushed and satisfied.

Max loosened the strap on from around her hips and let it drop to the floor. Then, she climbed onto the sofa, joining Rosa. She pulled her over her body and they laid, with Rosa on top of her, her head between her breasts, resting sideways.

Max ran her fingers through Rosa's hair, with her eyes fixated on the ceiling above.

"Does my age bother you?" she asked.

Rosa smirked into her chest. "No. I've never felt this safe nor desired anyone more than I desire you."

Max's chin moved against her head. She smiled warmly into her hair. "I feel alive again. I know I haven't spoken about it before and I appreciate you haven't pressed for it, but I should be honest with you, my ex-wife cheated on me with the very person who introduced us."

Rosa lifted her head to stare into Max's face.

"I fear not being enough for you. I also vowed never to let anyone break me like that again. So, if you're not sure—"

Rosa put a finger to her mouth. "I am sure," she nodded, and Max believed the sincerity in her eyes. "I'm in love with you," Rosa said. "I have been for as long as I can remember. I love you, Max."

Max smiled; she didn't think she would be able to love anyone again after Caroline. Her emotions were worn, she didn't think she had any more love in her to give, yet here she was, completely lost to Rosa who showed up at her doorstep and changed her life.

"I love you too, you know. Move in with me, properly. You and Bailey." she said, and Rosa's eyes widened in pleasant surprise. Immediately, tears began to gather in the corner of her eyes. Tears of joy. "Move in with me, Rosa Martinez. And let me love you, every day of my life."

Rosa laughed, sniffling sobs. "Yes," she nodded. "Yes, Max Moore, I will move in with you."

Both women laughed and Rosa pressed

her mouth down on Max's in a firm, long kiss.

They paused to look into each other's eyes. Giggling, they buried their heads into a fresh kiss.

EPILOGUE

2 YEARS LATER

Rosa and Max watched the monitor intently as Doctor Lillian Foster ran them through the ultrasound. The gelly felt cold on Rosa's belly but Max held her hand.

"That's our baby, Max. It really is." Tears were in Rosa's eyes.

"We did it, beautiful." Max smiled lovingly at her.

"Would you like to know the sex of your baby?" Lillian smiled at the couple.

"You can tell already?" Rosa asked excitedly and looked questioningly to Max who nodded and squeezed her hand.

"Yes, absolutely." Lillian said confidently.

"Then YES! I really really want to know." Rosa smiled widely, her big brown eyes expectant.

"She's a little girl." Lillian pointed to the monitor.

Max leaned in and kissed Rosa's face that was frozen in fascination. "I can't wait to meet our little girl, baby. You'll have to get thinking about names."

"I already know what I want to call her." Rosa smiled conspiratorially.

"Oh, you do, do you? First I have heard of this! What are we going to call her?" Max smiled wryly.

"We are going to call her Valerie after your Mom. I know how much you miss her and how important she was to you. I think she would be really happy to know that our baby was named after her." Rosa looked intently at Max for her reaction.

Max smiled with tears beading in her eyes. "Valerie," she repeated. She leant over and kissed Rosa's belly lightly. "I love you, baby Valerie. I'll do anything for you. I'll always protect you. I'll spend the rest of

my life loving you and your Mommy,
Valerie."

ROSA LOUNGED on the sofa with her laptop
determined to finish the first draft of her
next novel before Valerie was born. As her
belly grew, she found it more comfortable
to sit in a lounging position to write rather
than at her desk.

There was a knock at the door and the
dogs both barked. Diablo barely rose but
Bailey rushed around barking.

"Shh babies, it is ok. Quiet now." Rosa
heard Max opening the door and signing
for a delivery.

Max walked into the living room carrying a big box. The muscles of her arms
bulged in a tight black T shirt.

"It's for you, baby. I think I know what
it is."

Rosa's eyes widened in anticipation and
she sat up. "What?"

"Come and open it."

Rosa knelt on the floor and opened the
box. Inside shone piles of books. Her

books. Her second novel, *The Beauty of Her* by Rosa Martinez which would be available to buy very soon.

"OH MY GOD!" Rosa smiled widely and picked one of the books out examining the cover and flicking through the pages. "This is my second novel. I'm totally doing it!"

"You totally are." Max smiled and picked up a copy.

"I want you to sign a copy for me. I'm so proud of you, baby. You've come so far. You deserved all the success and acclaim of your first book and I have no doubt that *The Beauty of Her* will cement you as a real talent to watch out for. This one is exquisite. I can't wait to sit down and read it in paperback."

"You've read it a thousand times," Rosa laughed.

"And I'll read it a thousand more." Max smiled and kissed Rosa deeply.

THE END

FREE BOOK

Hey! Thank you so much for reading my book. I am honestly so very grateful to you for your support. I really hope you enjoyed it.

If you enjoyed it, I would love you to join my VIP readers list and be the first to know about freebies, new releases, price drops and special free *hot* short stories featuring the characters from my books.

You can get a FREE copy of Her Boss by joining my VIP readers list : https://BookHip.com/MNVVPBP

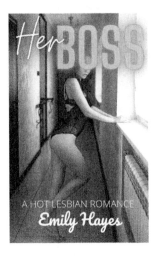

Meg has had a crush on her hot older boss the whole time she has worked for her. Could it be that the fantasies aren't just in Meg's head? https://BookHip.com/MNVVPBP

Eva Perez is the CEO of one of the biggest and most successful companies in her industry in the US. She has everything she could ever need or want in life. She is confident she doesn't need a girlfriend to complete her.

Most women fall at Eva's feet, so when a young woman turns up for an interview with her, who seems completely unphased by her power, Eva is intrigued.

Madison is captivating and exciting to Eva and sparks fly between them right from the start.

Will Madison ever be able to melt Eva's frosty heart?

mybook.to/TCEO

Thank you for reading! Lots of love, Emily x

Printed in Great Britain
by Amazon